DAISY BELL

DAISY BELL

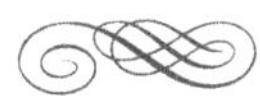

A Novel

J.K. PETRIE

Contents

PROLOGUE

Confined by gravity and free in mind, I walked that plane where my humanity never ceased.

Before the world ended, I lived in a small apartment with my grandmother. It was warm and comfortable, full of a wide variety of knitted things, guarded by kitschy porcelain angels who insulated the warmth and safety of our home. Their faces seemed especially cherubic every time I awoke from one of my many nightmares. Judgmental, even. But welcoming, regardless.

The apartment had only one bedroom, and it belonged to my grandmother. Though it bothered me as a child, I gained an appreciation for my sleeping situation as I grew older. When I rested at night, I always sank deeply into our ancient brown couch, flipping the rainbow of crochet that perpetually rested on top of it over my body. Doing this always provided a comfort so bone deep that I'd fall asleep in seconds.

Here is something that I've realized since everything changed. There is absolutely no feeling in the world quite like being surrounded by the lingering scent of a warm dinner that now fills your belly, ribs a bit sore from the laughter you shared with someone you love, legs tired from a long day at the menial yet exhausting job you took (You know—the kind of job that's merely meant to fill the liminal period between childhood and adulthood while you look for something better, but it overstays its welcome for too long to be considered "liminal" anymore), and finally, after such a long and rich evening, crashing on the old couch that has cradled you since you were just a child. See, other children had stuffed animals, blankets, sweaters, even…I had that couch. In fact, I had a whole apartment, even. All of it felt like one big comfort object. It took on its own essence. It had its own life. Intuitively, a child feels that a comfort object is alive although she logically knows that it is not. That's how I felt about the apartment. Still feel, really.

Anyway. The only feeling that even comes close to that is the swell you get in your chest when you are on your way home, it is raining outside, and you can see the orange glow of your apartment's window breaking its way through the deep blue landscape as if it is a beacon of safety. If it's during the right time of day, the smell of everyone's dinners cooking coalesces into one warm aroma, the streetlights hit all of the puddles just right, and you may have a small prize for your loved one clutched in your fingers. It could be a trinket for their collection, a dessert, ingredients for the dinner that you will cook for them. Something small. Something meaningful.

When I was young, I loved to participate in all of the joys of life that I possibly could. I had long since learned that it is short. I have now learned, at my bigger age, that the reasons why life can be so short is *because* of overindulgence in its joys. Sometimes they are not truly "joys" in the first place. Sometimes they are mirages that we chase out of desperation. This nuance, however, was lost on me for a very long time. I'd been overwhelmingly, painfully drunk, and overwhelmingly, painfully sober. I also knew the euphoria that both states of existence had the potential to hold. I had objects of passion to the point of obsession. That passion rooted from rage or love or lust. From immense grief.

Sometimes, I hoped to be the object, and often my wish would be granted. Through a series of partners and predators, some like vultures, some more like hawks, I learned that being *the* object felt better than being *an* object. But being *the* object, I now know, is a very dangerous game.

In the beginning, there was nothing.

In a beginning, there was nothing.

Though I have that knowledge now, it took experience to gain it. It felt special to be *the* object as a fresh teenager who still had the narcissistic and deeply buried desire to be one of the pin-up girls in the posters on my boyfriend's wall. It was a girlish desire to be a princess, I think, a trinket to be placed on some pretty boy's shelf and worshiped. Really, I guess I just wanted to feel loved. Was I wrong for mistaking that simultaneous reverence and degradation for the way that I was meant to experience affection and care? For digging desperately through all of the sickness and pain to find just one scrap of love? Do you blame me? I hope you don't. Or that if you do, you can forgive me, regardless. I don't know what's my fault and what isn't anymore. You be the judge.

Those relationships only started to feel wrong to me when my "*the*" changed to an "*an.*" I failed to see the myriad ways that all of them were doomed from the very start. The article that came before the word "object" was never the problem. The noun itself was. Unfortunately, that was my label. *Is* my label. *Has always been* my label. Literally and metaphorically. Long before my world ended. Long before I learned what I know now. It is now too late to change what I am. *Object.*

And the voice was the subject.

It started on my eighteenth birthday. The voice explained to me that it has been passively observing me for my entire life. I knew nothing about it. Rather than talking about itself, it chose to talk about me. It told me things about myself. Some of them were things that I did not know before, or things I didn't particularly think were true, not even after the voice would tell me them.

It was wrong, what they did to you.

If you did this, you would look quite a bit prettier.

That outfit looks nice on you.

I asked the voice if it were me, if it was just another way my teen self-centeredness was manifesting. I felt uncomfortable with those comments being thrown my way from inside my own head. It didn't *feel* like I was the one saying them, but I supposed that the voice had to be *some* aspect of myself. Some kind of weird Freudian narcissism. Every time I would ask, however, the voice would tell me no and would refuse to elaborate any further.

It lived alongside me. Strangely, the voice did not even speak to me in my own language, but I inherently understood its words as if it were prewired within me.

The language of God.

For my own comfort, I chose to believe it was a normal experience to hear such a voice. Still, I never discussed it with others. Perhaps it was some kind of taboo, some kind of open secret, like when I got my first period and I thought that something was wrong with me. Nobody had ever told me about it before. Despite that, everyone gets one, I learned. Regardless, something inside of me knew better than to bring the voice up with anyone else. It was quite passive and harmless, anyway. It felt more familiar as the years went by. It tried to influence me quite often, but I can't say that it really worked. I wondered, even, if it was a weird way that my relationship trauma was manifesting. At times, the voice sounded somewhat like a jilted lover. *Is this something dissociative?* I would wonder. *A maladaptive way that I'm coping?*

Still, I said nothing to anyone. The most knowledge I had on "hearing voices" came from movie depictions of psychosis. Not the most accurate. I didn't want to seek any more knowledge outside of that. Therapy would hurt. I feared pain. I feared the truth. I feared gaining any more unsavory labels.

Object.

I have learned since then that the voice is in fact *not* like a period, not like facial hair or stretchmarks or masturbation, not even like passive suicidal thoughts or active suicidal thoughts or the absolute depths of mental illness. The voice is not something that many experience and few discuss. Sure, some people hear voices, but only I have heard *the* voice. As for why I was chosen, I still don't know.

Supposedly, God chose Mary because of her purity. I know I am not pure. God chose Abraham because of his faith. I am not faithful. Perhaps I was chosen for my vulnerability. Or my body. The God that chose me is animal, privileged, wired to conquest and colonize and control, particularly what is physical—what he can see right in front of him.

Maybe I was just at the wrong place during the wrong time. Maybe something about me was inexplicably attractive. Maybe it was the fact that he was watching me through what was essentially a one-sided mirror, developing a parasocial relationship with me. And he knew that I was vulnerable. That made me worthy of taking. I just needed to be made physical.

There's no point in overanalyzing it, I guess. What's done is done.

I only have one request for you—think kindly of me. I didn't ask for this.

I

CREATION

I think that it was early autumn, if that means anything.

At the time, I was working at a local deli. I spent my days making sandwiches, filling sauce bottles, sweeping, mopping. Incredibly mindless work. I didn't see that as a bad thing, necessarily. Being able to zone out so often and think of other things was pleasant. I'd long mastered the art of orienting myself away from reality.

I thought that I might be promoted to supervisor soon. As I walked to the store for my opening shift, feeling the cool breeze, inhaling the earthy smell of dead leaves, I wondered if I wanted to get ahead of the game and quit my job before that ever happened. This is something that my grandmother might have clicked her tongue at disappointedly and referred to as *self-sabotage*. I thought of it as a breakup before things got too serious. If I was going to commit myself to a job, it was not going to

7

be at a deli. Nor at the fish factory, or a cafeteria, or as a cashier at the music store. I wanted something bigger, which obviously required some credentials. Credentials that I did not possess.

I'd saved a decent amount of money, but not nearly enough to afford going to school. I'd taken a few classes at our local community college, but I knew that I had no shot when it came to a four-year university. I didn't even know what I wanted to study, for one. Something to do with natural sciences, maybe? Biology? What kind of job could I even get with that? For two, I barely scraped by in high school. I would have been the last person to be considered for a merit scholarship of any sort. My best shot would be pulling the "dead parents" card in an admissions essay to receive financial aid. Even my grandmother had hinted toward that option before.

But I couldn't. I'd always refused to use them as a sob story. Not that I was offended by the idea of it. I wasn't interested in protecting their honor or their sanctity or something, nothing like that. *Not that they had any honor to protect,* I thought. I was aware that sounded cruel and calloused, but I didn't mean it in a derogatory way. It was simply the truth.

I supposed that my resistance to telling their story was because it left an important question unanswered. What did I have to show for it? My parents dying, I mean? I was far from a success story. I didn't contribute back to society in any meaningful way. Sure, colleges love it when applicants go against the odds, somehow; and God knew that I had plenty of odds. I didn't go *against* them, though. I moved with them. I didn't thrash against the tide. I passively let it carry me back to shore over and over and over again. What was the point? Could I overcome the small waves? Yes, easily. But they'd always turn into bigger waves along the way.

And either way, I knew that I'd end up back on land.

I hummed as I unlocked the store. My humming turned into a loud grunt when I heaved the equipment I'd need for the day onto the counter. As I did this, I became uncomfortably aware that a big part of my refusal to do anything more with my life was complacency. I liked going home after work to my grandmother. Going on dates that I knew would never go anywhere further. I never grew out of my love for cheap thrills and childish comforts, and I never grew out of my repulsion to responsibility. As I matured, I'd just learned how to take advantage of those comforts more carefully, how to avoid getting hurt in the process. And that almost made it *boring*.

At least it was familiar.

Even more than every other activity I consumed my time with, I loved pretending to be stupid. It felt like I was getting one over on somebody. It was also a way to protect my ego, I supposed. To keep myself from being vulnerable. At one point, long ago, I did it to entertain myself, to play with whoever I was courting. The Machiavellian nature of it had long since dissipated. It became a form of protection.

You're quite the seductress.

I inhaled sharply. No matter how long I lived with the voice, I never did get used to it interrupting my thoughts. There was a stinging pain in my fingers. I dully looked down. I'd cut them open on the tomato slicer, my blood combining with the fruit's acidic juices. Crimson liquid poured out from underneath the tomatoes, nearly blending into their watery orangish juice. I blinked.

"Fuck," I whispered. "Do you ever shut up? Do you have to distract me while I'm at work?" Tears of frustration squeezed out of the corners of my eyes. I hated the sight of blood. As I searched the room for our first-aid kit, I thought about some other things that I hated. I hated meat. I hated the way the meat at the deli came prepackaged and pre-sliced and soaked in its own juices. And the plasticky chemical smell that emanated off of it when you opened it up. I hated how I was treated like a piece of meat. Pre-sliced, pre-packaged, shelved up for sale. With a sense of *fakeness* that everyone pretends is natural. I wrapped my fingers in gauze until the bleeding stopped. It would leave a scar, but it didn't look deep enough to necessitate stitches. "I'm not a seductress," I said out loud.

The voice was silent.

I hated the way that none of the bandages were really water-proof, regardless of what the package said, so I'd have to wear rubber gloves when I did the dishes. I hated that water would in-evitably get inside the rubber gloves, anyway. I hated that I had to do the dishes. I hated that I had to work. I hated that things cost money. I hated that I just couldn't muster the willpower to want any more for myself than this.

...There's more for you in store.

I scoffed. *Okay, asshole. And who are you?*

I felt smug when I was met with silence. I knew that the voice wouldn't answer.

A frown crept across my face. *Normal people don't act this way.*

--

"What happened?" My grandmother's brow was furrowed in concern as she ran her thumb across my fingers.

"I cut myself on the tomato slicer at work." I avoided her gaze. "It was an accident." The fact that I even had to clarify was deeply embarrassing. Still, she did not look away from my face.

"Hm," she muttered. "You been clumsy, lately."

"I'm always clumsy."

"You sure it's accident?"

I felt some of the hot rage that coursed through me as a teenager every time my grandmother sent me down this line of questioning. I didn't react to it, but it served as a vestigial reminder of what our relationship used to be like. Strained, to say the least. I felt ashamed that it was still latent within me. "Yeah."

"Okay." She sighed. "I believe you."

I still didn't look her in the eye.

"I don't think you crazy," she clarified gently. "Just making sure. You know?" Somehow, she always knew my exact anxieties. It could be as frustrating as it was soothing. As a child, it made me feel *too* seen. Naked, almost. As an adult, it was more appreciated than not.

After a beat of silence, she continued speaking. "Time for make dinner." She turned away from me and started shuffling toward the kitchen. She had a funny way of physically removing herself from the situation every time it got too weird, every time the air felt too thick. She especially had a knack for making the situation awkward, then diffusing the awkwardness just as quickly as she brought it about. I think it might be a talent that all old women possess.

"Time *to* make dinner," I corrected her softly, slowly pacing behind her. She turned around and poked her tongue out at me.

"And how many languages *you* know, huh? In this house," she said, "time *for* make dinner." She grinned slyly. "Just like time *for* you to get out of kitchen." She smacked my arm playfully and began to ignore me in that way only old folks can get away with, humming to herself as she took a bag of carrots out of the refrigerator. I laughed and sank into the couch. Everything was okay again for the very last time.

—

Suddenly, it was dark. I had fallen asleep. I missed dinner—I could still smell it lingering in the air. I heard my grandmother snoring in her bedroom. Most prominently, I felt a sharp pain throbbing right between my eyes. I attempted to slip back into unconsciousness, thinking that it would be gone by morning. This did not work. For the next couple of hours, the sporadic sleep I caught came in bursts of vivid and confusing dreams that heated the inside of my skull until I was forced to awake again. It was as if my eyelids were forcibly snapped open every time I tried to go back to sleep. Overlapping whispers crowded my brain, all frantic.

A denial-of-service attack is when a legitimate user cannot access a system. This is because it is maliciously overloaded with illegitimate traffic until it can no longer respond or crashes.

Hospital? Grandma?

Fuck

and the bolt goes right through the cattle's brain right through it and the cattle dies painlessly but this is not painless oh no

sleep—fuck you're so annoying

mom

dad

After a few minutes of this, one resounding voice spoke over all others.

Walk outside.

Its tone had changed. It was more human, more evolved. It was now working in complete separation of my own consciousness rather than feeling as if it were rooted into it. Its vague suggestions and attempts at influence became demands. Finally, it was acting, a benign affliction turned malignant. Out of all the stimuli swirling in my brain, it was strangely the only one that soothed me. So, I followed its commands.

Carefully, I snuck past my sleeping grandmother's room. Everything in my head was so loud, I felt a strange worry that the volume of my thoughts could somehow wake her up. I opened the door slowly, the sound of its hinges nearly as deafening. I avoided all of the creaky floorboards. I always joked that I was as familiar with that house as I was with my own body. Every little feature that could get in my way—doorstops I've stubbed my toes on, items around corners, things like that—had long been memorized and accounted for.

But my jokes about familiarity with my grandmother's apartment were no longer truthful. I was less familiar with my body at that point than I was with most things, let alone my home. At least the home felt like mine. My body did not. It never did, to be frank, but the voice's sudden activity made it more true right then than ever before.

I stopped thinking about that. I could not afford to dissociate right then. It could trigger a panic attack. If my mental state got any worse, I might have done something that would awaken my grandmother. That was the last thing I wanted. It would be impossible to explain why I was going out so late. I knew that I would be far too incapacitated to lie to her. She might even try to take me to a doctor or something if she witnessed how delirious I was. Maybe she would think I was drugged. Maybe she would imagine that I'd had a secret night out on the town and that I'd been roofied. I didn't want to worry her that way.

Nothing in my own head made sense. I couldn't string a single thought together. The only thing that I could understand, the only thing inside of my own brain that made any sense at all, was the voice. So, I had no choice but to follow its instructions.

The next thing I knew, I was in the elevator headed downstairs. I couldn't really remember getting there. All of the different locations that made up my journey are now just flashes in my memory, everything in-between grey and uncertain. Like constellations.

When I got to the lobby of my apartment, I rushed through it and pushed the doors open with a flourish, the cold air crisp and welcome against my face. I found myself wishing that my brain could experience that same sensation. I imagined that my mind was an overheating computer.

Keep walking. I innately knew where to go, just like how I innately understood the strange language that the voice spoke to me in. I let my legs take me there (though I can't say I truly felt I had a choice) until I had walked through the urban landscape for hours. I felt as if my body was no longer mine, and I simply allowed it to do the work that my brain was commanding of it on its own. I eventually found myself at the edge of the city, but my legs did not cease. The sense of danger that came with walking alone in the city was replaced with the stark countryside's eeriness. Oddly, I didn't have any run-ins at all when I walked through the urban area. I didn't even see another living soul. Additionally, I felt oddly indestructible. Safe. Like there was no possible obstacle that could get in my way. Ironically, this, in itself, made me feel afraid.

My feet carried me beyond dirt paths and fields of dewy grass despite the pain that was shooting up into my thighs from my ankles. The pain inside my skull still felt even worse. I thought I might die. *Is this what they call a manic episode?* My suspicions felt confirmed when I realized I was standing inches away from the edge of a cliff.

Alright, the voice said, *look up. See the stars? Touch them.*

"How?" I whispered aloud. When I heard how foreign my own voice sounded to me, I winced at how little control I had over my strange behavior. *Dissociation, for sure,* I thought to myself.

Try.

That was my moment of truth. Underneath my blind faith in the voice, I felt the weight of the reality of the situation—that I was in the middle of nowhere, atop a ledge I did not entirely remember arriving at. That I was about to see if I could "touch the stars." It was so similar to the numerous tragic psychotic breaks written about in newspapers that I struggled to believe it was happening to me. Those were things that happened to *other* people. Things that *we,* as people who had a typical perception of reality, could not understand. Things that happened inside of heads that we thought of as so far from ours that there was no way we could ever truly comprehend why they did what they did, no way that we would ever do the same.

But here I was. About to do what I was about to do. Able to *make sense* of what I was about to do in a gut-feeling sort of way, even if my logical mind was screaming for me to stop. But there was nothing I could do to stop myself. It was going to happen. Just like it had happened to many before me. And just like them, I would be thrown into the category of *atypical,* sick, an "other" from the people who consider themselves "normal." I supposed that's what people do to comfort themselves. Convince themselves that there's no way they would ever be subject to the same mistakes that the people who are "different" from them make. The reality is that anyone can be driven to do anything, under the right conditions. This was proof.

Do it.

I looked down past the edge. The night made whatever lay at the bottom invisible, but it still looked like it was at least a 20-foot drop. I backed up and focused on the sky above me instead, praying that it was a weird dream. Perhaps I should have sought out help about the voice earlier.

But there was no time for regrets. It was too late for that.

As soon as the correct neuron fired, I took off sprinting toward the edge and jumped, reaching my arms toward the night sky.

There was no drop.

I floated.

My heart fluttered. I was flying. All of the pain I had collected in my body and carried with me throughout my lifetime seemed to melt away, too heavy to stay attached to me, forced to remain on the ground. My fears and earthly worries could not come along with me. *I could fly.*

Tears streamed down my cheeks as I desperately reached toward the stars. I hadn't ever been anything special before. All my life, I was orphaned and forgotten, only really having my grandmother as a source of stability, always knowing that she was impermanent and that I would one day be left all alone. Finally—finally, I had accomplished something God-like, something significant. There was no need to look down ever again.

Almost there, the voice said encouragingly.

My body approached the twinkles of light, warm and playful. They almost looked like they were swirling around one another, playing chase, innocent and welcoming. My mind reverted to childhood. As a kid, I had hours to look at the stars for as long as I wanted to. As an adult, I had to feel restricted in the world's smallness. I rarely got the chance to so much as look up at the sky. There was so little time to stop and take in the beauty of the world. I had to savor the moment whenever I was able to do so. I was finally put in a position where I could feel wonder for the world once more, forever falling upward. I remembered what it felt like to look up at my kindergarten teacher, a kind giantess. To look up at the glow-in-the-dark stars on the classroom's ceiling during naptime. Her slow and patient voice echoed in my mind. *Shoot for the moon. Even if you miss, you'll land among the stars.* That's what I needed. Slowness. Endless possibilities at my disposal. Unfortunately, my childhood was cut short far too early. I was herded into a singular fate before I was ready. At last, I got another taste of the slowness and vast freedom that comes with getting to be a child.

I realized I was approaching a darkly painted ceiling. There was no infinity despite what I had been led to believe.

I wanted to *make* infinity. I wanted to break it.

No, the voice said, not unkindly. *Look closely at the star in front of you.*

I did. I noticed that not only that star, but all the stars, were merely strings of LED lights attached to the ceiling I wanted to destroy so badly. Small, puny, even, always nearby. Not natural. Constructed by somebody else. I was closer to the wonders of my world than I thought I was.

Upon hitting the ceiling, I finally decided to inspect the landscape below me. Everything seemed so fake! The city below me was small and plastic. I was bigger than all of it. Seeing it all at once made me feel a deep admiration for my home. It was a profound appreciation for the smallness of it all. Cozy and tight knit like my grandmother's apartment.

Touch the star, the voice encouraged.

I reached out and pressed the tip of my finger to the warm bulb.

The night turned blindingly white.

I blinked my eyes rapidly. My floating feet became flattened by a smooth surface, but I was too stunned to pay attention to the gentle bodily sensations surrounding me. My back pressed against something. My eyes closed, but I could still only see that same pure whiteness. Nothing felt real. As my vision came back into focus, the white settled into something slightly less intense, slowly faded into shapes, took on various shades.

I was in a room. Every surface was pearly and luminous. Perhaps "room" was the wrong word. It felt more as if I woke up in a shiny box. I was lying on a hospital bed. I realized that I had been unconscious for an unknown period of time.

"Hello?" I nervously gripped my elbows and pulled them into myself. I was speaking in the language of the voice. My tongue naturally fit around the words I never dared to speak aloud.

The language of God.

I was never the especially pious type, but I still decided to take my best guess. "...God? Have I died? Mom? Dad? Are you here?" For a few seconds, there was only thick silence. Then I heard a chuckling voice break through the still air.

"I'm no god, in the Christian sense." A door in the room slid open and a man in a suit entered. He was followed by a group of people who were dressed more like me. That is to say, they wore casual and comfortable clothing. They all looked as if they'd never slept in their entire lives. A tense aura of exhaustion lingered around them. I almost felt tired just looking at them. All of the people in the room looked ever so slightly...*inhuman.* I recognized them as members of my own species, but their bone structure was different. High cheekbones, huge owl-like eyes that burned into your soul. Although they looked uncanny, they looked unconventionally, hauntingly beautiful.

"Who are you?" I asked meekly.

"My relationship to you is closer than you think." He paused, as if he was thinking carefully about what he was going to say next. Then he shook his head. "Not from a spiritual standpoint, though. If you define 'God' as a holder of life, a controller of worlds, then...well, yes, I suppose I would fall into that category." He grinned. "But that's quite the loaded term, don't you think? And my power is in no way mystical. Purely science." When he said the word *mystical,* he half-chuckled, half-spat the word ir-reverently. When I stared at him blankly in response, he cleared his throat and continued, changing the subject. "I believe you've named me 'the voice.' I mean, you could have been more cre-ative!" He smirked at his own joke.

I didn't laugh. I glanced at the crowd behind him. None of them laughed, either. They were too preoccupied staring at me in wonder.

"...But you're not my creator," I finally responded.

He smiled and inhaled sharply through his teeth. "Well...yes and no. I *did* cultivate the conditions that led to you." His eyes wandered across my body before meeting my own again. "What were millions of years for your world were mere months in mine." He slid his hands into mine. "But waiting for you felt like an eternity."

He moved forward as if to kiss the back of one of my hands. I pulled them away from him with haste, shocked. I was far too surprised about what I was learning to entertain his freshness. "I'm..." I paused. I was speechless. "Please...explain everything. I'm so confused."

He looked offended for a beat before letting out a low laugh. "Of course you are. I'm happy to." He sat down on the floor of the room and crossed his legs. To see such a well-dressed man sit on the floor criss-cross applesauce as if he were a child would have been humorous if I weren't so afraid. I joined him.

"It's truly quite simple. You are from a pocket universe that exists within *my* universe. A pocket universe that I created. I first began the project five years ago. Rather than going through the trouble of cultivating the conditions for billions of years of evolution, allowing your world to germinate from a big bang or primordial soup, I chose to replicate my own planet as it existed during the beginning of the Stone Age. See, I took a more humanity-centric approach to my project. Inherently flawed, I know, but I would have been more than a bit disappointed if I cultivated all the conditions for intelligent life only for humans- or human*oids*- to never exist. That's why you and I look ever so slightly, yet fundamentally, different. Neat, huh?" He chuckled. "What can I say? I just love people."

"And you replicated fossils, too? So after all this time, after all our scientific advancements, the fundamentalists were kind of...well, *right*? Evolution *didn't happen*?"

"Well, evolution is real in *my* world. To be fair, I misled the people living in *your* universe by copying my own world's conditions, so of course the evidence would lead the people in your world to come to that conclusion. But not everything lines up perfectly between our worlds. Far from it! You'll learn to adjust."

"Learn to adjust?" I repeated. I looked down at the ground. A deep pit formed at the bottom of my belly. "What do you mean, 'learn to adjust'? I want to go back home, eventually."

The group of scientists behind him shifted their feet in discomfort. He looked at me with slight sympathy in his eyes. His tone became apologetic. "My dear, you don't understand. What was formerly your 'home' no longer exists. I've ended the project. When you came into existence, I was fascinated with you. I wanted to be there alongside you. I chose to slow down my own perception of your world's time *just so I could take in every detail of you. And as you grew...*" he sighed dreamily. "Well," he continued with a bashful tone, "I found myself falling in love."

"Falling in love," I dryly repeated under my breath. *"Ending the project"? What the hell does that mean?* I stared hard into my hands.

I realized that they were not my own.

"This...is not me." I glanced up at him frantically. "I'm not in my own body," I said, hushed and panicked. I couldn't believe the very words that were coming out of my own mouth. In fact, they were so unbelievable that my body was numb to the gravity of their meaning. It was too incomprehensible, too impossible.

But it was true. Oddly levelheaded, the man responded, "For you to survive in this universe, we had to make some adjustments. Your old universe's conditions are far different from mine, so I engineered a new body for you that could more easily survive here before you arrived. It must have felt only like seconds to you between being in your universe and being in mine, but we transplanted you into your new body while you were unconscious."

I continued to stare hard into the ground, intentionally placing my hands behind me so they were outside of my field of vision. I was in too much shock and denial to cry. My new body couldn't even begin to process the news he had given me. Could anyone? Is this something that humans are equipped to handle? Am I even capable of coping with the existential questions and grief that this was bound to cause in me? It felt unreal. I expected to wake up any moment.

He lifted my chin and gazed into my eyes. "That was the most intensive and revolutionary project I ever attempted. It was my life's work. I ended it all for you. I wanted you to be here with me."

A soft chorus of mushy cooing and *Aaaw*'s erupted from the small crowd behind him.

"My grandma's gone?" I asked, dread flooding my chest at the very suggestion.

"And everyone else. I know it must be jarring, but if it helps, it's not like it was a painful ending." He stood up and turned to the group, his cheerful demeanor unwavering. "Alright, team. Project Metaworld has officially sunsetted." A collective and exasperated cheer emerged from the crowd. I stayed on the ground. I stared into the tile hoping, again, desperately, that I would wake up, hoping something would happen to make everything make sense.

I never did. Hoping wouldn't help. Praying wouldn't either.

The language of God. And God is in love with you.

God loves his children.

2

GOLDEN CALF

The billionaire, as I learned he was, gently placed his hand underneath mine as he helped me into a heavily guarded vehicle. It was akin to a futuristic limousine. Not only was he unusually young for a billionaire, but he was also the world's richest man. "I want to celebrate you," he said. He kissed the back of my hand and wrapped his arm around my shoulders. I let him. My anxiety, quelled enough to only be surface level by then, unraveled and pulsed in waves throughout my body once more. I tried to feel attraction for him, but it refused to be summoned. Trying to muster together that kind of feeling felt like trying to strike a wet match or play with a Ouija board by yourself. My nerves dampened all other possible feeling. So did my skepticism. I knew that my safest bet would be to play along with whatever would please him.

Feeling attracted to him would please him.

I simply couldn't do it.

I rolled down the window of the vehicle and looked at the sun. It was brighter than it was in my original universe. Everything was ever so slightly different. The feeling of the air coursing through my lungs felt a little bit harsher than it did before. Whether it was because of my new body or the different air quality or altitude, I did not know. But it was still different. I didn't like it. It felt like a dream.

Everything was far too unforeseeable for me to feel any comfort whatsoever, having just arrived in this new universe and already having to take a giant plunge into the public eye. I was the creation of the world's richest man. His romantic partner, too. Just yesterday I had come home from work to my grandmother sitting at our janky kitchen table, pouring tea for both of us, her ever-comforting aura and unconditional love brightening the entire apartment, beautifying it. Just enough to warm the small world that we shared together. To heal me, whenever I needed it. I still didn't feel sad about the fact that she was gone. I hadn't had any time to process it. Aside from that, my new situation was far too inconceivable to feel real, regardless. Really, I still expected to wake up and see her standing in the living room's doorway. She would inform me that I had been screaming in my sleep. Not the first time it's happened.

The billionaire interrupted my train of thought. "Do you know what they're calling you?" he said to me. "The alien girl. My little alien girlfriend. Isn't that cute?"

Slowly, I turned my head to face him. I could not manage to make my face look anything other than blank. He didn't seem to notice.

"From another universe," he continued. "Do you have any idea how amazing you are to the people here? You're unique to them. Everything about you..." he trailed off and looked me up and down. Already, I noticed that he did this a lot. Getting used to his wandering eyes would be yet another thing I'd have to add to my mental list. "You look ravishing," he finished.

I felt indifferent to his compliment. The beauty standards, too, were different in this new place. Before we left, I had been treated like a doll, my face painted over and my hair tightened into a style that was foreign to it, clothes chosen for me and tailored to my body to hide some features and accentuate others. I didn't think of my hidden features as undesirable until then. I didn't consider the features that they chose to accentuate particularly attractive, either. All of this was done to help me conform to this new world, to make me more acceptable under the public eye. I supposed that I must have looked beautiful based on the reactions of the cosmetologists once I was finished, but I didn't grasp what "beauty" in this new world actually entailed. I had no choice but to trust the people who did, just like I was going to have to trust others about everything else. I didn't like the vulnerable position that this put me in. In fact, I hated having to trust anyone at all. Throughout my life, I'd been forced to adopt the attitude that if I wanted something to be done right, I had to do it myself. If I didn't want someone to hurt me, I simply needed to prevent them from getting too close.

But the billionaire knew everything. Had heard all of my thoughts, knew my deepest vulnerabilities and insecurities, knew all about my darkness. I had no other choice but to trust him with this information.

Eventually, the car stopped in front of a museum. It was a large and simple building made mostly out of glass. The only opaque pieces that broke up the endless clarity were metal support beams and a few places in the vast building that had no windows, only matte blackness. They contrasted intensely with the surrounding reflective and open glass. I wondered if it was for customer privacy reasons, copyright reasons, light-sensitive artworks, or maybe something else. Either way, those spots seemed as if they were there out of necessity, not aesthetic. Whatever architect designed this building obviously intended to make a statement with its complete openness to the world; Tall, big, intimidating, but ultimately delicate and vulnerable. I supposed that the strange windowless spots in the building were the best compromise between functionality and form.

If you looked carefully at the museum, you could see that even the walls inside of it were mostly glass, allowing an outside viewer to look right through it. Two people on either side of the entire building would be able to see one another. Anyone inside the building, too, is exposed, as if they are art pieces to be observed and picked apart in themselves.

I noticed the building before I noticed the spectators congregated outside. There were hundreds of them. I felt the urge to hide my face from them. "Don't worry," the billionaire whispered to me through a smile. "The party's inside. It's very private. I'll introduce you to some friends of mine."

His arm awkwardly lingered around my shoulders as we stepped out of the vehicle and slowly walked toward the entrance. I wanted to speed up, but it was as if the billionaire was insisting on making a spectacle out of us. He soaked in all of the attention with pleasure, continuing at a leisurely pace, stringing me along with him as if I were his pet. The spectators also seemed to regard me as if I were a statement piece, an accessory, a novelty item. Maybe my insecurity or lack of understanding on how the people in this world worked caused me to have that perception. Either way, I could not bring myself to look at the crowd. Any reminder that this world was not my own introduced a new pang of nausea to my stomach, and their big piercing eyes did not help. I could still feel them burning into our backs whenever we entered the museum.

The inside of the building was dark, small spots of ambient lighting only serving to highlight the pieces on display. This meant that the natural light from outside, or lack thereof, did most of the legwork. It was difficult to see the pieces from outside of the building, but I could now tell that it was a museum of *modern* art, specifically. Or was it? *Is this what they call modern art, here?* For a second, I felt more existential dread creeping beneath my skin as I again pondered the conventions and status quo of this brand-new culture that I would likely never fully immerse myself into or understand. I expelled those thoughts from my mind for the sake of preventing a public breakdown. Or putting it off, at least. I had a foreboding feeling that one would happen, eventually. But not here. Not in this giant glass box, not where everyone both inside and outside would be witness to it on full display.

The anxiety I felt ceased a little as I allowed myself to take a bit of satisfaction in what was still similar between my new world and my native one. The artworks easily looked like they could have come from my own world. Some paintings were mere bold and bright strokes across canvas, the colors so saturated that they burned into my retinas. Others were soft and blurry portraits of girls, yellow and brown-tinged, a little ruddy, their come-hither looks inviting the viewer in. Looks of desperation that could be confused with seduction. Maybe the other way around. Girls that ignored the viewer flirtatiously. Evilly, if not flirtatiously. Abstracted figures of women that danced nude in the sun. Men charging into war, men charging into sex. Never exposed, though. Nakedness was only for the public display of the feminine form. As it was in my own world. Unfortunately ubiquitous.

My focus switched from the portraits to the glass wall.

They were still staring.

So I switched back. I lost myself in the paintings of the girls again. *No matter what,* I thought, *humans are destined to create for the sake of creating and build temples for their creations.* I took comfort in this.

Creation is the language of God.

I wanted to get a better look at all of the works and read their plaques. The billionaire had been clinging to my arm the entire time, talking to some other men in expensive-looking suits about things I did not understand. I gently walked away from him so I could examine the art more closely. When I leaned down to read one of the artist's blurbs, I heard the billionaire chuckle from a distance. "She's a mysterious one, isn't she?"

A voice to his left responded, "Sure seems that way. Is she adjusting well?"

I pretended I couldn't hear them as I continued my exploration.

"Hmmm. She'll get there."

"How does she know our language? Surely, her kind's language didn't develop exactly how ours has." A loud and booming laugh erupted from the disembodied voice. His tone became infantilizing when he uttered the phrase *"her kind."* I couldn't help but flinch. Flustered, I tried to play it off.

I heard a coy smile in the billionaire's voice. "I taught her without her ever knowing it."

"You sure do enjoy playing God, don't you?" Another loud laugh.

Frustration shot down from my head. Fear shot up from my stomach. They intersected in my chest, created tightness, birthed anxiety. At that point, I actively tuned out the conversation instead of pretending to. I didn't want to think about the conversation behind me. I didn't want to be a part of it. I didn't want to be around anyone who would talk about me that way.

Object.

Despite the museum's unique architecture, it was still much like any other building I'd been inside of since arriving to this new world. Geometric, overly smooth. Unfortunately, that meant that the sound of my heels clicking against marble easily betrayed my attempt to sneak away. I didn't care. I needed to get rid of that tight feeling before it exploded outside of my body. Fast. Everyone could see me. Soon enough, I would spiral into a panic in front of the hundreds of people who were observing my every move. *I just need to make my way to a bathroom, or something.*

I glanced around desperately and quickly found one of the odd places where there were no windows, just matte darkness. It was a hallway.

When I made my way down it, I heard rapid footsteps gaining on me. I powerwalked. I kept my chin up. I overcompensated in fear that I would lose composure. They still caught up to me. I felt a hand grip my forearm and I whipped around. "Let go of me."

"Where are you going?" The billionaire sternly looked me in the eyes. His tone reminded me of the way a father would scold his daughter. With disgust, I yanked my arm away from him.

"They're treating me like I'm an object. Like I'm not a real person. I don't want to be here anymore. Actually, I didn't want to be here in the first place." My words ran together and became uncontrollably shrill. I was too upset to be self-conscious.

He gave me the same sympathetic look he had given me when he informed me that my world had ended. I could see it up close that time. It looked forced, upon closer inspection. Maybe he'd even practiced it in the mirror. Maybe he rehearsed the suave speech he would give me beforehand. Maybe he didn't expect me to reject the stupid pick-up line he decided to lead with.

"Waiting for you felt like an eternity," My inner voice mocked.

His dumb fucking face when I pulled my hands away from him. The only expression he's given me that looked human.

I took some satisfaction in that.

His insincere, robotic facial expressions made me think of a powerful man practicing a public statement he must make about a scandal, finding the best way to make himself look as good as possible. *The pure inauthenticity.* I filled with even more rage merely at the thought of it.

After a couple of seconds, he broke my feverish stream of thoughts. "Baby..." he whispered.

I snapped. "Don't call me that. You don't know me like that," I spat.

He blinked in shock. I cowered away from him instinctually. After a tense pause, he spoke again. Slowly, this time. "I know you better than anyone else *ever* has. I've been watching you for your entire life!" He sighed and closed his eyes. After a moment, he opened them again. The fire in them had dissipated. "I'm sorry they were talking about you that way. They're only treating you like an object because they're putting you on a pedestal. You're the alien girl. You're amazing." He tenderly put his hand to my cheek. I looked downwards and made no effort to move it away.

"For now, the amazement they feel toward you is...well, superficial. But they'll get to know you. They'll get to see what *really* makes you shine." He took my forearm again, gently this time. He slid his hand down my wrist until it met with my own, interlocking our fingers. I sighed and chose to swallow my anger. What use did it have anymore?

"Come with me," he muttered warmly.

He led me further down the hallway and turned a corner. The talking and laughing voices echoed and became more distant. I realized that it was my first time alone with him. I supposed that it was better than being a spectacle to hundreds of complete strangers, despite the uneasiness it made me feel for just the two of us to be alone together. Either way, there would be uneasiness.

Like a square peg in a round hole.

"Where are we going?" I asked cautiously.

"A surprise," he responded in a playful tone. He turned to look at me and pressed his finger to his lips. He winked. I startled myself when I let out a giggle. A small bubble of frustration popped in me. *I don't like him. Why am I laughing?*

We approached the door that I previously thought led to a bathroom. "Stay right here," the billionaire whispered to me. He pulled a key from his pocket and pressed it into the knob, fumbling with it for a few seconds. He entered the room and shut the door behind him. After a few beats and a little shuffling, he spoke again, his voice muffled. "You can come in now."

My chest swelled with awe when I walked inside. A huge table with rows and rows of little plastic buildings on top of it stood in the center of the room. Faintly, I could hear city ambience echoing through hidden speakers. The sounds of *my* city. The room was housing a mini replica of my hometown. All of the walls were painted midnight blue—a warm blue, purplish, welcoming, not like the unforgiving cold vastness of the sky that I usually envisioned when I thought of nighttime. Rows of little LED lights were attached to them, meant to resemble stars. The stars I reached out and touched the night prior. I walked up to a wall and gently placed one of them between my pointer finger and thumb. *Warm, small, encased.*

These walls are unbreakable.

When I dissociate, the sky always looks like a giant wall.

"I commissioned it just for you. Nobody else has seen it, nobody ever will." He stood behind me with his arms crossed. "So you don't ever have to forget where you came from."

Every single detail that I could remember from my past was present. I recognized the deli across the street from our apartment building. I didn't *love* working there, but I missed it, regardless. It always smelled like freshly baked bread in the morning.

All of the cracks in the sidewalk that I'd always carefully stepped over were present. My high school was there, carrying all of the gravity that it always had. Everything was where it should be.

I started at the replica of my apartment and slowly paced my way around the table, getting a close look at all of the little buildings and landmarks. When I looped back around again, I kneeled to the ground and looked into the miniature version of my grandmother and I's window. Inside of it was a miniscule sculpture of her sitting on the big brown crochet-covered couch, knitting.

My elbows hit the floor. The breakdown I had been putting off had finally arrived. All of the shock that shielded me from crying was gone all at once. The reality of the situation hit me like how my body should have hit what lay beneath the cliff. It was pure gravity. I cried softly for a few seconds, then my sobs got louder and more guttural until they sounded like the screeches of a fatally wounded animal. My screams hurt my own ears, but there was no way for me to control them. All of my surroundings were greyish blurs, melding together, colors chasing each other wildly like how the stars seemed to swirl before I reached out to touch one. It felt like I was stuck in a vortex. For a moment, I felt as if I were one of the abstracted girls I had seen in the paintings earlier, inhuman, all violent strokes, painful and bold and messy and stuck right in the middle of an otherwise blank canvas.

The billionaire rushed to my side and fell, half-tripping, to the floor next to me. I did not see his face. I couldn't really comprehend anything outside of myself, in fact. I barely even registered it when he pressed my head into his chest. He stroked my hair feverishly and harshly. It reminded me of the way a toddler might pet a cat. I muffled my screams using his body and grabbed for his shoulders, clawing blindly and wildly, embracing him in my complete desperation for connection. I felt drool and tears pool around my face and soak into his shirt. I kept screaming hysterically as if all of my pain could be purged through my voice. As if it could be absorbed into the billionaire's body and disappear forever. But it would keep coming up again. And again. And again. I was experienced with trauma. I knew that it was just an endless game of mental whack-a-mole. But it was a lot easier to act as if it could all be screamed out, vomited out, bled out, cried out, drowned out, poured out of some sort of orifice. It can't. The sickness stays. The damage is permanent.

The billionaire's hand met the small of my back. "*Shhhh,*" he whispered.

He knows me better than anyone else ever will.

3

DELILAH

We spent what must have been hours in the room before I composed myself well enough to leave. It didn't feel like hours, though. It didn't feel particularly short, either. Actually, it was as if my body had deviated from the concept of time, entirely. When I had my breakdown, I was in a vast void of absolute nothingness. *The big bang birthed three dimensions of space and one dimension of time.* That's a quote from an old textbook I read in high school. It's funny, the random things your brain remembers in the midst of panic, all the odd bits and pieces of memory that really latch onto you.

During my breakdown, I did not feel as if there were a linear dimension of time. I didn't feel three dimensions of space, either. Everything coalesced and mixed and burst forth and back at the same time, sensations melding into something bigger and space becoming one-dimensional, infinitely dimensional, antithetical to the very concept of dimension, too. Points in time converging. Little girl in a woman's body. It was not a new feeling. This paradigm of lawlessness and dissociation dictated the way my body addressed many things. Panic bubbles up in response to the smallest of triggers. Panic is a choleric infant. You don't always know why she is crying, and you don't always know how to soothe her, either.

The makeup so carefully applied to my face had rubbed completely off onto the billionaire's chest. The cosmetologists had laid it on so thick that the front of his shirt looked like an expressionist painting of an anguished face. This might have been darkly humorous to me if I were not so drained. Upon noticing me staring, the billionaire looked down at his shirt. His face twitched in displeasure, but he buttoned up his jacket without a word.

There was no rush to leave the room. He made the effort of staying with me until nobody could tell I'd ever been crying. He tried to crack jokes, point out different things in the replica to distract me, even play I spy with me until I was grounded enough to finally face the world again. I didn't laugh at his quips or enthusiastically play along with him or anything, but I appreciated his effort. It helped me calm down a little bit more.

When I was ready, the billionaire walked out first. He stood by the doorway and tried to gauge if anyone was nearby. He popped his head back into the exhibit and whispered, "The coast is clear." He gave me a small, sheepish smile. I left only a lingering glance at the exhibit before I followed him.

As we walked back out of the hallway, the billionaire checked his watch and made a sucking sound through his teeth. "I...know this probably isn't the best time to tell you," he said, "but I'm ending this event with a conference in about 20 minutes. Have you ever done any kind of public speaking?"

I was taken aback. *I thought this was supposed to be a date.* I bit my tongue and felt my lip quirk into a small sneer as I became self-aware of my own girlish *neediness.* I didn't even *like* him. Besides, the social conventions that make up a "date" in my own world might not constitute a "date" in this one. "No," I responded honestly, anxiety collecting at the bottom of my gut.

He threw his head back and laughed, detecting the nervousness in my tone. "Hey, don't worry," he said. "You just have to show up. You're not going to do any speaking. I'll make sure of it."

--

The conference would be broadcasted live. It was the one part of the museum event that would be available to the public. It was some kind of motivational speech, tailored to appeal to techies and make the hearts of STEM majors everywhere soar. I tried to envision what the nerdy high-school aged boys who looked up to him must look like, watching all across the world at once. Only boys, though. It was unfortunately difficult to imagine a young girl looking up to a man like him. Though I'd only known him for a day, I could already tell that he was something of a chauvinist. I looked at the empty stage where the billionaire would soon stand, thinking back to the artwork of women I had seen earlier, flirtatious, evil, soft, unscientific, brains malleable like the clay they were sculpted from. *No, not a good representative for female scientists.*

It was something of an "official introduction" to the world, the billionaire said—he referred to the rest of the museum date as a "casual meeting." I was thrown off by what he considered "casual."

Of course, he drilled me on etiquette before we entered the auditorium. I think he was worried that this time, I would have a more public outburst than what had occurred earlier. We'd narrowly avoided being the center of attention. *If you converse with anyone around you, don't talk about your past, it's off-putting. Don't get personal. Be friendly. Not too friendly. Listen. Be engaged, not too engaged.* I remembered about half of it. That was fine. I didn't think anyone would want to talk with me much, anyway. Regardless, I can't say I wasn't happy about the opportunity to socialize with others without the billionaire glued to my side, even if it was to briefly exchange some polite greetings.

The billionaire soon stepped on stage, but my anxiety still made it feel like all eyes in the room were on me. I ran my cues through my head. They, too, had been stressed to me before I was allowed to take my seat. Like I needed anything else to memorize. *The billionaire will say something that you can't quite understand because you are so close to the speakers. It's okay, though, because he will gesture to you and grin as he says it. It's something about how you are his best accomplishment, his magnum opus, his most artfully crafted piece, whatever. Your ears will ring with anxiety. You will stand up, wave, curtsy, sit down. Stand up, wave, curtsy, sit down. Stand up, wave, curtsy, sit-*

I felt the seat next to me shift, a small sigh exiting somebody's lips as they sat down. I glanced over and smiled instinctually.

The person did not smile back. She was a woman, probably close to my age, maybe a little older. Maybe she wasn't actually any older than me, though—it could've been her mature demeanor. She seemed slightly annoyed, maybe uncomfortable, with the small amount of space between the two of us. She had dark curly hair, a light brown complexion, and a tired expression. That, too, could have been a reason why she seemed so mature. Something about her was immensely intriguing to me. It could have been my loneliness, or perhaps there was something about her that drew me in. Her dark eyes, traced with bruise-colored circles, pierced into me with a trace of question.

Wait. Fuck. Am I supposed to smile at people? Is that normal?

"Hi," I blurted out.

"Hi," she responded dryly. Her tone had an intimidating finality to it. I did not make an effort to continue the conversation. *Just exchanging polite greetings.*

Soon, the lights dimmed. Her dark eyes turned charcoal.

As I anticipated, I could not understand most of what the billionaire was saying. I could get the gist from his tone, though. As he went through his introduction, it was bold, confident, even somewhat smarmy toward the audience, I recognized. Only someone of his stature could get away with being so damn *smug. Maybe he was advised to really lean into the whole "father figure you never had" thing for the sake of his young male audience.* I almost smiled, then felt a flash of guilt. *C'mon. That's mean.*

I waited for my cue, anxiety filling my body by the second as if I were a glass being filled with water. I don't remember standing up and curtsying—my body acted as if it were in a trance. What I do remember, however, was the shock that spread through my body after what I heard when I sat down.

"And here's to my head engineer and best friend, who's been

with me through it all. We go way back, ladies and gentlemen! Veronica, please stand up."

The woman next to me rose. She was still tight-lipped, her demeanor strictly professional. She turned to the audience and bowed, giving the billionaire a single nod. Her expression still did not change when she sat back down.

As the billionaire began his speech, I glanced over and spoke lowly. "Best friend, huh?" I attempted.

"I'm *his* best friend," Veronica replied. "Not sure if I'd say he's mine." I chuckled. She did not.

"I'm surprised we weren't introduced during the party," I said. "Since you're the head engineer, and all. I wonder why that is?"

Veronica shrugged. "Busy. I was the one doing the behind-the-scenes work to make what you call 'the party' happen. And honestly, I see no need."

I was taken aback. "You don't see a need for us to be introduced to one another? You must have worked on...the project, what was it called..."

"Metaworld," Veronica responded. "And most of that was the billionaire's pet project. I was hardly involved."

"Well," I said, "even so, I think I'd like to get to know you. We'll be in pretty close proximity, right?"

"No," Veronica responded shortly. "I highly doubt it. And really, I'm not interested in getting to know you any further."

I was at a complete loss for words. I didn't understand. Was I being socially awkward? Was there something I was missing? There couldn't have been. There was some kind of distrust in Veronica's eyes. Something vaguely hostile. What had I done? I'd barely said anything to her—shit, I was trying my best to be her *friend.* I glanced up at the billionaire on stage. He had no idea about the conversation happening right in front of him. His mouth was moving. Bass-filled gibberish was exiting the speakers. There was only one conclusion I could draw from the way Veronica was treating me. With conviction, I looked at her again.

"Veronica," I said. She glanced over at me. Those intimidating eyes. I swallowed hard and continued. "Veronica," I said, "Did you and the billionaire...?" I trailed off. Veronica had a look in her eyes that warned me not to continue, a fire sparking. Through all the noise and stimuli, I could still almost feel her breath on my skin. I decided not to let her discourage me. "You had something. Clearly. Maybe *have* something. That's why you don't want to interact with me, right? Be honest. Are you—"

"I am not jealous, and I could never be jealous of you. He and I are business partners." Veronica interrupted. Her tone was gravelly and low. "Jealous of such a one-dimensional, flighty..." she grunted in frustration, turning away as she interrupted herself. "You know," she said, "You fit perfectly into a man's idea of what a woman is like. You are every negative stereotype rolled into one. And your idea that I must not like you because I am *jealous* shows that more than anything else."

I fell silent, red-hot embarrassment and anger flushing my cheeks. *One-dimensional and flighty?* I thought. *I never went to college, sure, but there's no way I come across as...dumb.* The tension between us was thick. "You know, I just thought that maybe—"

"That maybe I worked my ass off since I was twelve to get the position I have now for a *man?* For *him?* Please." Veronica picked at the threads on her seat as she spoke. A nervous tic. I'd hit a nerve. "Do you really think I haven't heard that before? Unlike you," she continued, "I don't exist for him."

She, too, had hit a nerve. I didn't *ask* to be brought into this universe. I had a whole life behind me before he decided to insert himself into it. A whole life ahead of me, too. I knew I was my own person. I was tired of being treated like I wasn't, like I was incapable of being anything more than an ornament for the billionaire to decorate himself with. "I'm not an extension of the billionaire, you know," I muttered. "I'm a being with my own thoughts, emotions, feelings." I paused, took a deep breath, and mustered the bravery to tell her what I was about to say next. "I can't help the position...I've been put in."

Veronica looked away and continued picking at the threads. The billionaire's speech droned on, mere background noise behind our interaction and all of the tension behind it. Tears glossed my eyes, but none fell. As the billionaire completed his speech, the audience swelled into applause. In the midst of all of the noise, Veronica turned to me. "You're not what I thought you were," she offered. An expression I could not read was written across her face as she was swept up into the crowd, all exiting the auditorium in a buzz.

Girls ignoring the viewer with an air of mystique, if not evilly nor flirtatiously.

--

It was pitch black outside. The saffron-toned lighting hanging over the artworks reminded me of the warmth of a streetlight on a dreary day. I felt sure that the artworks looked even more gorgeous when the sun was setting outside. Unfortunately, I missed the opportunity to bear witness to that. *Maybe another time.*

Very few people were left in the museum. All of the guests had gone home already, only leaving workers who were there on professional business. Whenever I would come into contact with one of the employees, they would silently quirk an eyebrow at me or the corners of their lips would twitch a little. I'm sure that they were just exasperated and not much in the mood for catering to other people anymore. If this were my own world, I might have smiled at them in response. I didn't, though. Aside from not having the energy myself to keep up a facade, I still didn't know how things worked here, yet. I knew that it was best to stay as far away from social interaction as I possibly could for then. Especially after Veronica.

When we reached the lobby, there was a group of five or six bodyguards waiting for us. In contrast to the museum personnel, they were completely stone-faced, quiet, and unreadable. The billionaire marched toward them with purpose, as if he were a commander about to give his soldiers an order rather than a man on a museum date. He glanced back at me and muttered something to them. They nodded and walked over to me, making two rows on either side of my body. I hoped that my face did not betray my annoyance. All of this extra security was already growing cumbersome.

After he directed his order, the billionaire made his way to the museum's gift shop. I followed him and tried to ignore the huge men looming over me. To distract myself, I admired the building's architecture. I hadn't seen the gift shop yet. It was oddly expansive, built in the style of a department store. There were multiple floors—three, to be exact, all visible through the glass walls. *Is that unique to this museum?* I wondered. *Or is such a huge gift shop commonplace in this world?* My thought was interrupted when the billionaire turned around to stop me.

"You have to wait here," he ordered. I was put off by him directing his commanding demeanor at me, but nonetheless, I complied. As he walked away, I soaked in the weird liminality of the museum. I, again, yearned to see the sunset glimmer through all of the glass corridors. I knew that it would have looked gorgeous.

When I was in high school, I would fantasize about spending the night there. If I made it to school early enough so that I was all alone, I could imagine that I was in the midst of a zombie apocalypse. I'd entertain myself by thinking of all the different ways I would survive using my school's resources. I would think about using up the dry food stored in the cafeteria, growing fresh food using our agriculture club's resources, deliberate over what items in the different classrooms would work best as weapons...I could do that for hours. The museum had a similar zombie apocalypse-like liminality at night. Perhaps it was the scarce lighting. Maybe its eeriness was intensified further by the fact that everything in this new world was slightly different in ways that I could not always put my finger on.

This thought prompted me to ponder the liminality of my own body. The way that I perceived things must have also been different than before. Moving in the new body felt different overall, so far, but I became aware of the fact that I was sensing this world through different eyes, different touch receptors, different ears, a different nose. My consciousness, too, might be housed in a different brain. The Ship of Theseus flashed inside my head. I put it out of my mind before I spiraled into that rabbit hole of lost identity and personhood questioned. I could not afford to expend that mental energy. Only recently had I begun coming to grips with my new reality. Existentialist angst would only worsen that process.

I need to focus on right here, right now, what I can see right in front of me.

The entire time I was wrapped up in my own thoughts, the bodyguards made no attempt at conversation, only looking straight ahead as if I weren't there at all. Not that I was in the *mood* for conversation, anyway. Any attempt at icebreaking would have been a social faux pas—avoiding interaction still felt like the correct route. Still, it felt strange for all of us to remain so silent. The space that existed between me and the men standing next to me felt endless. *Our worlds were never meant to converge.*

About twenty minutes after he left me alone with the guards, the billionaire returned with a full shopping bag. "Come on," he said to nobody in particular. The bodyguards escorted us back to our vehicle.

"Why didn't you ever introduce me to Veronica?" I blurted out as soon as they shut the door behind me. I'd been waiting to ask him since the conference ended.

"Well, hello to you too," the billionaire said, half-chuckling. I stared at him. He cleared his throat. "I guess it just never came up," he continued. "Why do you want to know?"

Because she's the most intriguing woman I've ever met. Because I want to know what kind of man you actually *are, and I think Veronica would be able to tell me. Because I can tell that she doesn't think you're a fucking god, unlike everyone else. Because there is a potential for understanding. Because she would make me feel less alone. Because I think we could bond over the fact that we recognize you as a flawed person.*

Because I think we could bond.

"I'd just like to know about her," I said lamely.

The billionaire gave me a questioning glance, then laughed loudly. "I can see what's going on," he said. "Baby, you have nothing to worry about when it comes to Veronica and I. She's of the *opposite persuasion,* I'm pretty sure. Besides, she's married to her work. And you won't be seeing her, anyway."

I stared at him. *You don't fucking get it.*

"Okay," I replied.

"Anyway," he muttered awkwardly. He looked down at the bag of items he'd just bought, then at me. I could see his expression flicker, suddenly. That must have been the exact moment he saw an opportunity to change the subject.

He excitedly pulled me toward him. Shockingly, I found his touch a bit endearing. I could smell cologne on him and mint on his breath. Just a tinge of garlic, too. He must have chewed some gum to try to get rid of the odor. "Look, my love," he cooed softly. He pulled an array of items out of the shopping bag. One was an absurdly expensive bottle of perfume. There was also chocolate and some printed magnets of the exhibits that I studied for an especially long time. After examining the objects, I raised my head to look at him.

He smiled. "It's for you. It's all for you." He took my hand and squeezed it. "I gave you the world, and I'll keep giving you the world."

4

CHARIOT

We arrived in front of the laboratory. I found this rather odd —it was getting late, and I reckoned that the billionaire would have wanted to take me home so we could rest. "...Aren't you going to take me to your house?" I asked him.

"No," he replied simply. "We still have some work to do."

Something about his tone felt foreboding. A fresh wave of anxiety washed over me.

"And hey," he joked, "this is way more like my home than any conventional house. Yours, too!" He poked me and smiled.

The anxiety remained. His silliness was doing nothing to prevent how inexplicably unsettled I felt. I played nervously with the magnets and said nothing.

Once we entered the lab, the billionaire led me to yet another pearly white room. I supposed that this would be my bedroom. Temporarily, I hoped. By one wall was a white bed with a white metal frame. It looked old and worn. The paint on the frame was chipped, exposing the slightly rusted metal beneath it. It ruined the illusion of perfection and complete sanitized feel that the room would have otherwise had. It had a white pillow, white sheets...at least those looked clean. There was nothing else in there. I was shaking. I squeezed the magnets in my fist until the corners left imprints on my palms. The pink indents in my hands, the slight pain I felt from them, and the colorful artwork on the magnets were the only stimuli in the room that I could soothe myself with. I clenched my teeth and pressed my tongue to the roof of my mouth. Something did not feel right. I wished desperately that I could put a name to it, but much like every-thing else in this universe, it was too impalpable to describe. I'd always hated not knowing. There was a lot of comfort to be had in putting a name to a feeling, categorizing it, then tucking it away somewhere in your brain. It felt good to know that you're unhappy because you need more of a certain vitamin, that you don't like someone because they cheated on their boyfriend, that you don't like a room because it has no color inside. Being unable to rationalize a feeling has always been a living hell for me. Unfortunately, it happens quite often. My body knew things that I didn't.

I heard the squeaking of wheels approaching. The billionaire rolled a large cart through the doorway. On top of it was a complex machine of some sort. Like everything else, it was also smooth and pure white. Many parts dangled off of a giant, central piece, shaped like a box. All of them looked like electrodes save for a helmet-like segment of the machine. I look questioningly back and forth between the billionaire and the machine. The tightness in my chest made it a great effort to speak.

"I haven't named it yet," he admitted, "but I anticipated that it might be difficult for your new body to acclimate to the environment." He sat down on the bed next to me. We stared at it together. "There are many things that you will have to get used to. I mean, not to brag, or anything, but I'm quite confident in my abilities when it comes to this kind of science." He giggled beneath his breath. "That being said, I created your body from scratch. Its immune system, its ability to handle different objects and stimuli, is comparable to that of a newborn infant's. It needs to get used to the atmosphere, water, food, everything that you ingest." He casually stretched his arms over his head, stood up, and walked back over to the machine. He gestured to it as he spoke. "What this will do it help your body acclimate. It cycles the nutrients you need through your system and slowly exposes you to different particles and bacteria that you will be introduced to in your everyday life, reducing the chance of sickness and helping you build up immunity in a safe way. You'll have to wear it every single night for it to do its job properly. I promise it's comfortable, though. I made it especially for you." He put his hands on his hips and turned his body to face the machine, giving it a satisfied and proud smile.

Though he did not notice it, I was filling up with more disbelief and rage by the second as he spoke. I clenched and unclenched my fists repeatedly. My vision began to swirl. "So you're telling me that you destroyed my entire world only to transport me to a different body that can't even *function properly yet?*"

His smile fell. All at once, his expression shifted. He snapped.

He marched toward me and slowly leaned down, nearly pressing the tip of his nose against mine. I felt the urge to cower away from him. I suppressed it. This seemed to enrage him further.

Through gritted teeth, he hissed, "I *made* your fuckin' world. I'm trying to help you. I took you out of there because I *saw something special in you*. And right now..." his fists balled up. "It feels like you're proving me wrong."

I nervously gazed down at his hands. "I'm sorry," I whispered hoarsely.

His eyes burned into me for what felt like forever. I could still feel their intensity cutting through me when I looked away from him. Eventually, he looked down at the ground and composed himself once more.

"As I was saying," he continued slowly, "you'll have to wear the machine every night. Let me help you get into it."

With presumptuous nonchalance, he reached toward my shirt. I instinctually smacked his hand away and covered my chest. "What are you *doing*?" I shouted. I instantly regretted my reaction and cringed away from him.

I could see his face getting redder and his rage increasing by the second. This time, however, he closed his eyes, took a deep breath, sighed, and looked at me as calmly as he could possibly manage. He spoke even more slowly than before. "The machine monitors your heartrate, temperature, and breathing through electrodes that attach to your body in various places," he said. "I was going to attach them for you. You can't exactly do it on your own. This way, the machine will detect how much your body can reasonably handle without falling ill."

I was too afraid of pushing him over the edge to argue any

further. One more act of disobedience from me could have been what sent him over the edge. "Right," I sighed.

He allowed me to undress myself. This was the most privacy and grace that was extended to me. As he attached all of the different electrodes, I strained, with great difficulty, to prevent the onset of a panic attack.

Object.

I disgustedly pushed that thought out of my mind. I covered my face with my hands and breathed into them strenuously. *Close your eyes and think of anything else.*

I can't feel his hands on my body. This is not my body, anyway. It is not my body that he is touching right now. I am not in this body.

My mind kept returning to all of the times I had to be examined by a gynecologist. I required a chaperone every single time. Sometimes the doctors were understanding, sometimes they looked at me funny, sometimes their expressions were dry, lips tight, eyes glazed over, annoyed with the inconvenience. My grandma always offset their ire with a reassuring and empathetic smile.

I remembered the feeling of my grandmother's soft hand holding mine whenever I had to get a pap smear. She kept them well-moisturized; they were always supple, perpetually smelling of pomegranate lotion with a tinge of dish soap. Sometimes I would squeeze it. She would squeeze mine back and put her other hand on my shoulder. Distract me with conversations about work or school. Tell me about something funny she saw on her way to the supermarket.

That was always how I got through OB/GYN appointments or any other doctors' visits that were too invasive for my comfort. So, I pretended that my grandmother was there with me, making her intense maternal love evident to me by squeezing my hand. In my mind, she was next to me, assuring me that I was not an inconvenience, pulling my attention away from a rude doctor's judgmental looks using gossip about women in her knitting circle. "Remember Rhonda?" she would say. "Let me tell you what she found in husband's sock drawer..."

By the time he was finished setting the machine up, only a bedsheet and various different electrodes and wires covered my body. My fantasy of comfort vanished. The ghost of my grandmother's memory was gone. Only the billionaire and I were in the room. I noticed then that the machine restrained me to the bed, and I felt like crying.

He dusted his hands off. "Well," he said cheerfully, "that's all done! I'll get you out of it in the morning." He put his hands on his lips and smiled down at me.

"I can't move," I blurted out. "I've only known you for a day. I'm scared," I pleaded. I was afraid that I would start hyperventilating at any moment. "How do I know you won't hurt me?"

The billionaire's smile turned to a sardonic smirk. "You don't," he said.

Then he left me alone in the room.

I listened to the soft whirring of machinery and stared into the device's glossy finish. I could faintly see the reflection of the face that was so foreign to me.

That body was not mine.

5

FALL OF MAN

After he hooked me up to the machine again, the dreams I had that night were not kind to me.

I was plagued with night terrors. The kind of night terrors I hadn't had since I was a little girl.

Flashbacks of violence. Of death in sleep. Of *murder* in sleep.

The sound of my mother's screams through the smothering of a pillow.

The overbearing and ever-louder silence that proceeded them.

The sound of my father's sobbing and screaming when he understood the gravity of what he had done.

The self-inflicted gunshot afterward and the wound it left.

The final and loudest moment of silence.

6

TOWER OF BABEL

I awakened to a pair of eyes watching me. I gasped but managed to stifle the scream that should have followed. It was the billionaire staring at me from the doorway. "You scared me," I said.

He sighed and softened his calculating, sharp gaze. "You were talking in your sleep," he said. "Screaming, too. About the things that happened to you as a child, I think." He shook his head and started moving toward me. "I love you, darling. I'm so, so sorry." He took a knee by my bedside and unhooked the machine slowly and methodically. "I hope you know I'll always be here to protect you."

I did not respond to him. I never told anybody about what happened to my parents. Only my family knew the truth. Even through all of the emotional manipulation I had been through in my past, I knew that it was not a good idea to ever provide anybody with that kind of ammo—and for what? Sympathy? As I saw it, that was the last thing that I needed.

Obviously, I had a lot of feelings on what happened to my parents, but other people's attempts at comfort and compassion only served in making me feel deeply uncomfortable. Knowledge of that aspect of my childhood felt like one giant piece of a puzzle that made every other fucked up thing about me make sense—not only that, it made my brokenness undeniable. Who wouldn't be irreparably broken after their father killed their mother, then killed himself? If I didn't share that information with people, it wouldn't color their vision of me. Maybe they would think I was just an introvert or shy or a worrywart or that I gave too much of myself to people, all for no particular reason. Just traits. Those traits being defined by my "mommy and daddy issues", however...*that* felt frustrating and hopeless. If they're just personality traits, just the way that I am, then they are transient. Changeable. It means I have the potential to come out of my shell. If they're a result of my parents dying so violently, then those traits are no longer thought of as traits. Now they are side effects of an unfixable chronic disease of the mind. Side effects of memories that are impossible to erase. That's why I always felt so against the idea of attending therapy. Though I'd never admit it out loud, I can't shake the feeling that therapists are hardwired to provide unshakeable labels. I am unable to handle having a permanent label put on my personhood. I can't risk it. I can't risk what that would do to my psyche.

And after all, it's not like therapy helped my parents.

It was incredibly jarring for somebody to already know all of my secrets. In fact, I was surprised that after seeing everything

I've done for my entire life, all of my absolute lows, the billionaire still had interest in me that was akin to the parasocial relationship a boy has with the pretty girl next door. Of course, that's before he actually gets to know her and sees all of her flaws up close. But everything the billionaire knew about me changed nothing about his infatuation with me. *Does that make it true love?*

I couldn't help but shudder at how well he truly knew me, inside and out. I've always struggled with grasping mathematical concepts, but this vaguely brought something else to mind for me. A fourth dimensional being, supposedly, would be able to take an egg yolk out of a shell without cracking it open. A fourth dimensional being would also be able to peer into a cross section of our bodies from all angles, see our insides without opening us up. Make things that are physically impossible and irreparable happen by flipping objects across a fourth dimension that we, as third-dimensional beings, are unable to see. The billionaire was a bit like that. Able to read my thoughts. Able to see my literal insides, too. Must have, at this point, seen all of my viscera and selfishness and disgustingness. He warped my original universe, as well. Or my perception of it, at least. *So, I thought, he must love me. It must be...well, some form of attraction. Some form of love that maybe I don't fully understand.*

Maybe it's some kind of fourth-dimensional being love.

When he finished unhooking the machine, I got dressed. His eyes burned deeply into me as I did so, making discomfort pulse through my body and my hands shake as I buttoned up my shirt. After I finished, he clapped his hands together cheerfully. "There's an emergency meeting I have to attend today."

"Am I coming with you?" I asked. I half-hoped Veronica would be there.

"No." He paused, as if thinking of a way to articulate what he had to say next. Then he added, "I don't think you'll be leaving the lab too often."

My stomach dropped. "Why?"

"I don't think that the world's ready for you," he replied. "In fact, I think we only need one another. They don't understand you, anyway. Besides, we can always rent out a public space for the day if you want to go out somewhere that badly. We can have little date nights. I'll reserve an entire theme park just for us this weekend. How does that sound?"

I looked down at the floor and did not respond. Unbothered by my disappointed response, or perhaps just ignorant to it, the billionaire hummed to himself. "I've got to get going. I was supposed to be out the door ten minutes ago." He walked out, stopped, then backtracked into the room. He looked at me with an expression that was half concerned and half stern. "Do not touch anything in this laboratory. A lot of my projects here are works in progress. If you mess something up, something crucial to your existence, for example...I may not be able to help you." He gave me a lingering stare before he left the room again and closed the door behind him. After his footsteps became distant enough to be inaudible, I mindlessly fingered the magnets he had given me the night before. I eyed the bottom of perfume. *I don't even wear perfume,* I thought to myself bitterly. *He should know that, of all people.*

I'm in fucking misery.

After enough time passed, I became bored enough to open

the door to my room and warily wander the hallways. There was nothing to be wary of, though. They were empty.

The words that the billionaire said to me the previous night echoed through my mind.

How do I know you won't hurt me?

...You don't.

My body suddenly felt shaky and weightless from uneasiness. Sick fucking joke. If it *was* a joke.

I didn't get far before I scurried back to my room. Though he hadn't told me that I wasn't allowed to leave it, exactly, I was still in a hurry. I was immensely afraid of getting caught.

God, I thought to myself, *I'm so scared of this man.*

For the umpteenth time, I felt like crying again. I was terrified. Utterly terrified.

--

Hours passed. I thought it strange that I had no means of connection with the billionaire; no cell phone, no landline, not even a pager. I stuck all of my magnets to my imperfect metal bedframe, attempting to cover all of the spots where the white paint had chipped away. When I became bored with that, I laid on the floor of the blank room and pressed my legs against the wall like a child. I vacantly stared at the ceiling and pretended that there were glow-in-the-dark stars pasted to it.

Will I just be a hermit from now on? Can I be anything but a hermit anymore?

I'd always struggled with introversion that toed the mentally unhealthy side of things. At first, I was confident that my reticence was just in my nature and did not originate from any kind of social anxiety. Over time, it became more apparent to me that

I really was experiencing immense nervousness over my capacity to interact with others. It deteriorated before I even realized what had happened or could muster the mental capability to reverse it. Even when I took that fact into consideration, that I was a homebody turned recluse, my restriction to that single room made me acutely aware of all the things I liked having the freedom to do. Going shopping, to the park, to the farmer's market, anywhere but this white fucking room.

This prompted a memory of the term "white torture." White torture is a tactic used by various state governments in which prisoners are kept in a completely white cell with white clothes, white food, no shadows, no noise, complete smoothness. Virtually no texture. In its attempt to convey cleanliness and technological advancement, this room came dangerously close to that. The pops of color that the artworks on the magnets provided combined with the chipped-away paint on my bedframe offered some minor form of relief, but they were incidental. They were prints of the paintings I had stared at in the museum—those infantilizing depictions of women, sexualized, child-like, nothing behind their vacant eyes. The billionaire bought me those magnets on a whim. The chipped-away paint was not an intentional detail. If it weren't for the magnets and the bedframe deteriorating, this room would come close to being a perfect way to passively torture me. Make me compliant, maybe.

Perhaps that's the goal.

I shook my head. The more likely answer was my initial suspicion. Cleanliness and tech. Probably nothing more than that.

But there's no way to know for sure. Is it really so out of his character?

I pushed the thought away.

After about half an hour of mulling over the decision, I chose to escape those unpleasant thoughts by leaving my room and exploring. The fear and suspicion I felt was being replaced with loneliness. I missed him. I felt the bone-deep kind of calm that comes after being punished for a tantrum when you're young. The kind that makes you miss your parents and long to join them for dinner downstairs.

The long hallways were blank and dark. The only thing that broke the endless walls of pearl were immense windows, but it was a gloomy rainy day. I could see the droplets crawl down the glass but could not hear them tap against it. *Soundproof?* I thought. White torture came to mind again, but I pushed that thought away, too. My brain felt like a finicky vending machine rejecting crumpled dollar bills. Or maybe my brain felt like a body. A sick, shaken-up body purging everything bad out of it from every orifice possible. My grandmother had advised me before to think of my own bad thoughts as clouds passing in the sky. *Just observe,* she would say. *Don't need to cling.*

I would think, *But where are they going?*

Nevertheless, the thought was gone. I pressed my fingertips against the window and marched forward, lazily dragging them along the wall.

I decided to give myself a mission. My task was to find a kitchen area. Aside from feeling rather hungry, it would give me a good enough excuse for leaving my room should the billionaire return too soon. I hummed under my breath. *Can I even eat normal food here, or has the billionaire been feeding me something different?*

I never did find a full kitchen, but I found a kitchenette that had a coffee machine and a plastic basket full of granola bars on the counter. I thought that sufficed plenty. When I made my way toward it, I nearly bumped into a woman who was exiting the kitchenette at the same time. As if I were compensating for the scream I should have let out earlier, I screeched right then. I was so focused on the task I had given myself that she caught me completely off guard.

The woman dropped two cups of hot coffee onto the ground. "Aw, shit."

"I'm sorry," I blurted out. "I'm so sorry. I didn't see you there."

She was already on her knees picking up the coffee cups. Her eyebrows were furrowed, and her lips were pursed in an indignant expression I usually only saw on children. Her youthful freckleface did not help with this image. In fact, her freckles were a highly saturated brownish orange. I could tell she went outside a lot. Though she had to be at least twenty-five years old, I thought that she looked like an elementary school tomboy in a lab coat.

"Be careful next time!" She looked up at me just as the words left her mouth. Her expression shifted. "Oh. Oh, fuck. You're the alien girl, aren't you?"

"I guess that's what they call me?" I chuckled awkwardly. My sheepishness did not seem to sell my charisma.

"I'm so sorry. I sincerely apologize." She stood up and brushed me off ungracefully. "The coffee didn't burn you, did it? I can't go ruining the boss's most prized possession." The last sentence had no trace of a playful tone. If anything, it sounded a little bitter and sarcastic.

"I'm fine," I insisted. I realized that this was the perfect opportunity to practice social interaction. "So, um. What's your name?"

"It's Nancy," she said. "Aren't you supposed to be in your room?"

I winced. *An "And you?" would have sufficed.* "Well, I g-got hungry," I stammered.

"He didn't take care of that before he left?" The corner of her mouth raised in disgust. "Typical." Her bitter and sarcastic tone was back. It was more intense, this time.

"What?"

Nancy suddenly became flustered, as if she had only just realized that I could hear her talking. She probably didn't mean to say that out loud. "I didn't mean- well- I hope you're not offended—"

"I'm not," I replied flatly.

"Just—" I heard sincere panic in Nancy's voice. "Please just don't tell my boss. Please?"

I smiled a bit to myself. She really *did* have a childish streak. "Find me something better to eat than a granola bar and we have a deal."

She grinned back timidly. "Sure."

Looks like I still have my charm.

"You know," she continued, "You're pretty human-like, all things considered, Alien Girl."

I was taken aback. The conversation was steering toward a weird direction again. "I am human," I replied. I was shocked by the uncertainty in my own voice.

Her eyes widened a bit. I probably wouldn't have noticed if I wasn't meeting her gaze so intensely. She cleared her throat and whipped around, briskly walking back to the kitchenette. She returned a few silence-filled seconds later with a roll of paper towels and leaned down to mop up all of the coffee she had spilled. I stared at her, still waiting for her to continue speaking. The sheer awkwardness was thick. "Well," she finally said, "I suppose at the end of the day, it's a philosophical question, isn't it?" It seemed as if she had carefully constructed her reply during those few seconds of tense quiet. Really, it felt like hours.

"I *am* human," I repeated.

"You...sure seem to have the self-awareness of one!" she said, laughing nervously. "And the functions, too. It's a bit strange that you need to eat at all. You know, we humans—" she blushed at her mistake. "I-I mean. *Our kind* tend to think of eating as a sort of inconvenience that connects us a bit too closely to the rest of the animal kingdom. When it comes to conventional society, especially *polite* society, as you've been exposed to the most..." the bitterness in her tone returned for a second. "Well, we have a desire to ascend beyond the flesh. It's what people aspire to do."

"What a calloused take to have!" I responded, deciding that the niceties I'd usually extend for a conversation with a stranger did not apply here. She didn't know it, but she hit a point that I was very passionate about. I was not angry, but perhaps I came off a bit too aggressive in my eagerness. "What's so wrong with a connection to nature? We *are* animals."

Nancy looked at me quizzically. Did I sense a touch of fear in her expression? "Who...who is 'we'?" She whispered, bewildered. I got a feeling that she was talking to herself out loud, again. She continued, more directly addressing me. "No. No, you're *not* an animal. Yes, *I* may be an animal, in the most literal definition of the term, but you?" She shook her head. "Not even close. *You* must know that, of all people."

It was my turn to be confused. "Nancy, I'm just like you." I reached out and brushed my fingers against her forearm. Remembering the billionaire's words, I said, "There's no need to put me on a pedestal."

She grimaced and backed away from me, looking at me the way you would look at a politician you know to be corrupt--with an expression that conveyed unease, disbelief, and a tinge of disgust. "No. We are *not the same*. I'm human. *I'm real, and you're not.*"

I stared at her. I could feel that my face was betraying the pain coursing through me.

"Look. I...I need t-to go. Let the boss know that I'm taking lunch, alright?"

"Nancy—"

She turned to walk away. I gasped when I saw her bump into a tall figure that neither of us had noticed during our conversation. She looked up at his face and let out a small gasp.

It was the billionaire.

"No need for that." The professionalism in his voice was deeply unsettling. It made him difficult to read. Slowly, he meandered toward me and wrapped his arm around my shoulders. Nancy stayed frozen in place, only her eyes following him. Ignoring her, the billionaire pulled me into him and looked down at me. "You could've told me that you're hungry," he said lowly and somewhat affectionately, as if he was speaking to his pet cat rather than a grown woman. *He'd been listening to our conversation for that long?*

With his hand on my back, he began walking me back down the hallway away from Nancy. He called over his shoulder, "And by the way, you're fired. *Nobody* treats my alien girl that way."

He looked toward me again and winked. A pit formed in my stomach.

I never saw Nancy's reaction.

I never heard from her again.

--

"I *told you* that people just don't understand you," the billionaire said through a mouthful of cheese. We were sitting on the floor of my stark bedroom, a greasy pizza box joining forces with my bedframe to disrupt the clean aesthetic of the area. It turned out that I *could* eat normal food here. *In moderation*, the billionaire emphasized. I was not sure what his motive was behind restricting what I could eat. As I mindlessly picked the pepperoni slices off of my pizza, the way that an overly neurotic first-time mother treats her newborn baby came to mind. I thought about the close familiarity that mothers tend to have with that small collection of tissue and viscera that so recently was a part of their own body. They cling to their baby with a desperation so strong, you'd think they're trying to absorb it back into their own flesh. A coworker of mine acted this way. She was a teen mother who made her child her entire world. No prepackaged baby food. Only the most wholesome of mush for her child. No formula, ever, no matter how difficult it was for her to get her daughter to latch, nevermind the thrush that she caught, and nevermind what a struggle it was for her to lactate. Of course, her helicopter parenting never ceased, and her daughter became quite rebellious as she grew older. The billionaire was like that.

Only the most wholesome of mush for me.

"I think she seemed nice," I replied, pretending that there were no thoughts bouncing around inside of my head outside of that. I grabbed an extra slice of pizza. The billionaire stared at my hand and furrowed his brow, but said nothing.

"That's your problem. You need to have more self-respect. She was *insulting* you to your face, darling!" There were those over-protective parent vibes again.

"Maybe she just didn't know any better," I said. I hoped that the kindness I was frosting over my tone would create the impression that I am innocent and unknowing. It was like heaping buttercream onto an artificially flavored and stale cake.

"That's your last slice," he responded snidely.

At that, we ate silently. The rage his comment made me feel waxed and waned in my body before finally subsiding.

I was exhausted. No need to escalate.

That small icing-like voice was now inside of my head. *Maybe he's just looking out for your fragile body's health,* it said. *Maybe he is just stressed. Perhaps compassion is the best route?*

Fine.

I broke the silence by changing the subject, hoping that the tension both of us felt would be relieved. "So," I said, "when am I sleeping at your house?"

He stopped chewing for a beat. "Probably not for a while."

"Why not?"

His face twitched. "I can't tell you, but I promise it's for your own good."

"Aren't I your girlfriend?" I said, speaking a bit more intensely than I intended. All of the rage that I had cast out earlier was germinating into my body once more. "Am I your girlfriend, or am I just another science experiment?"

He threw the pizza box across the room. "You're not coming to my fucking house. End. Of. Story." His tone was scarily dry. He stalked out, leaving me alone again.

So much for not escalating.

Tears welled up in my eyes. I wished that I could make sense of his turbulence. Predict it, prepare accordingly for it, do all the right things to soothe it. Understand what keeps this man who has so much power over me happy.

Is God meant to be loved or feared?

--

7

SONG OF SOLOMON

As he promised, the billionaire took me to an amusement park that weekend. Despite the uneasiness I felt due to our previous interactions, the billionaire seemed as if he didn't even remember or care about his outbursts. Perhaps he, too, was trying to distract himself from the tension between us or convince himself that it didn't exist. After all, what is one meant to do with the fact that they transported someone across universes only to be denied a fairytale romance? What was I meant to do, either? It was better for both of us to pretend it was working and hope that eventually, it actually would.

He held my hand as we strolled through the ghost town-like atmosphere of the area. He knew I had a fondness for amusement parks, as I was constantly spending what little money I had to go to them when I was still living in my original universe. What he failed to pick up on was that amusement parks were so appealing to me because of the way I could get lost in a crowd. There was nobody else there. Of course, that excluded the group of assistants trailing behind us for safety reasons, including Veronica (whose presence only made me feel more awkward.) I felt oddly exposed and strange, as if I did not belong there. He tried, in the least.

All I could hear were the sounds of empty rides running with nobody to carry them and the distant hum of vehicles on nearby roads. Oddly, the billionaire provided me with a comfort that I could not explain in the midst of our vulnerability.

"Isn't this great?" he asked me. "No lines to wait in. We can spend all our time here doing things we actually *want* to do." He chuckled. "And, of course, there's the privacy. Especially appreciated, considering the constant public and professional activity our situation requires."

I didn't *feel* very "private." Nonetheless, I gave him a forced smile.

"Which one do you want to ride first, my love?"

I thought for a minute. I was sure that there was a right and a wrong answer to his question, so it took careful calculation to decide what to say next. When the billionaire and I talked, it felt sort of like a dance, like a strict Victorian courting ritual. If I didn't move with his flow, I risked ruining the rest of the date. "Well," I said finally, "what do you recommend?"

His face indicated that that was the right answer.

"This park has one of the oldest rollercoasters in the world," he responded. He looked down at me and winked. "Want to have a historical experience together, sweetheart?"

I felt disgusted at the swell of affection in my chest that made me feel. What's worse is that it did not feel entirely compulsory.

"Sure," I grinned shyly. He kissed the back of my hand and led me to the ride in question.

As we walked, I tried to rationalize the odd feelings I was experiencing for the billionaire. A small voice in my head whispered, *Stockholm syndrome.* I ignored it. Much like the impulses I felt that resulted in jumping off the cliff in my home world, Stockholm syndrome felt like something shameful that could only happen to a brain different from mine. But really, I knew, anyone can be driven to feel, experience, or do anything. It's just about differing thresholds. I liked to think that adulthood erased every trace of potential I had to feel love from abuse. This couldn't have been true, but I wanted it to be. So it was.

My louder conscious mind was telling me that perhaps it was a good thing that I was getting used to the billionaire, that maybe this affection could be organic, true, fulfilling. Maybe it could turn into true love. Maybe—just maybe—the billionaire had more to him than his outbursts, and maybe there was something to love in him if I went in deeply enough. Maybe he was worth it. Maybe I could come to love him once I got to know him more thoroughly. I liked that answer better.

I'm ashamed to admit that I ended up having fun being taken to all of the different rides in the amusement park. Something about our date had me feeling similarly to how I did when I would be taken out by someone from my high school. There was excitement in knowing that there was the same underlying motive that went unsaid when it was just me going out alone with someone else. There's a lot of power in what is not spoken out loud. Usually, I was the one being pursued by the other. There, too, is power in holding the metaphorical stick with the carrot at the end. Making someone chase you, giving them a journey they must complete before they may finally claim their prize...Some might say it's somewhat of an old-fashioned feminine role, that it is objectifying and demeaning. But when I used my body as a tool without tying too much of my personal being and identity to it, it did not feel this way. It's just a hunk of flesh and fat and bone and skin. The other person could consume it without consuming me. When my body was entirely mine to give and take back, I felt powerful.

The billionaire, of course, was just a fill-in for my ideal boyfriend for then, and our juvenile courting ritual was a facade. He was someone I could project my *actual* desires onto so I could cope with my lonely situation. In reality, I didn't have any power at all. He was humoring me by taking me on a date, creating the illusion that he still needed to win me over and acting as if he couldn't do whatever he wanted with me at any moment. I was grateful for that small attempt at normalcy, at least. It made me feel just a little bit less vulnerable. I was still considering the possibility that he could become more meaningful to me in the future.

After all, do I really have any other choice?

He was in an especially good mood after I started to warm up to him. I still struggled to conjure up flirtation-- on some level, I did still find him repulsive—but he didn't mind.

He likes his women docile. He likes to chase.

He likes to hunt.

The small voice in my head was getting too loud. I snapped

out of my weird satisfaction with the billionaire and, once again, realized who I was and *where* I was.

I was essentially the billionaire's possession.

I was in a universe where nobody else in the entire world understood me.

This date was not an attempt to win my affection. He was trying to lull me into complacency.

"I need to go to the bathroom," I said suddenly. I was washed over with the need to get away from him, even if just for a few moments to collect myself. The smile on the billionaire's face twitched.

"Sure," he said. He took my hand and escorted me to the closest restroom.

When we arrived at the door, he stepped forward as if he was going to follow me in.

"...What are you doing?" I asked. I said it in a tone that suggested he was breaking the conventions of a traditional date, hoping that his desire to embody normalcy would override his urge to watch my every move. *This misstep can be redeemed if you follow my lead,* my tone said. *A reward is still available to you. Just let me keep the power for now.*

The billionaire's eyes burned into me. I had a bad feeling that his good mood might be eroding. He might have sensed the gentle suggestion in my tone, but if so, he gave no indication. "It's dangerous for us to be apart, darling. I insist on coming in with you. It's for your safety."

God, is he serious?

I coughed. "Uh, well. It's girl stuff," I lied. "Could you please just wait outside the door or something? It's embarrassing, you know." I paused awkwardly. "I'll be fine, dear," I said finally, feeling as if I had to force the last word out of my mouth. That was the first time I returned his habit of using pet names. The situation was dire, so it called for it.

Ever so slightly, his face lifted from his "moments-from-snapping" expression. I could see that it worked. He turned to Veronica. She hadn't spoken at all, quietly watching us the entire time. I didn't try to initiate conversation with her. I thought it would only make things even more awkward, especially with the billionaire right behind us. Aside from that, I got the feeling that things were tense between Veronica and the billionaire right then.

"Will you go in the restroom with her and keep watch? You know how determined people are to get their hands on my alien girl. I want to do all I can to protect her." With that, he shot me a stern glance.

Veronica jumped at the sound of her own name. "Of-of course!" she said. "Right away."

I can't say that I wasn't disappointed with this compromise. As much as I wanted to talk to Veronica without the billionaire's supervision, I wanted to be alone right then. I think that aside from wanting a break from the billionaire, I wanted the chance to try something. To figure out a way to escape, namely. Really, I didn't *actually* have any chance of succeeding at all, even if he *did* allow me to use the bathroom alone. Trying to run off would inevitably lead me right back to where I started. He's the richest man in the world; I am his possession.

Maybe what I wanted was the illusion of choice. I was *that* desperate to feel like a person. Such a small act of rebellion as sneaking away from the bathroom and running off, even if a happy ending to that scenario was impossible, would make me feel existent. Like I am not just an extension of him.

Or maybe this was a strange indicator of my preference to be chased. I am ashamed to admit it now, but the few times my past partners were not exceedingly and grossly obsessed with me, I would pick fights with them just to watch them get afraid of losing me. I needed constant proof that I was desired. A certain kind of abusive partner provides that proof constantly through their overprotectiveness and jealousy. When that's all you're used to, anything else just doesn't make the mark. Perhaps that explains my inclinations when it comes to romance. Perhaps that, too, explains why I liked the billionaire's all-consuming domination and hated it all at once.

These are things I will never say out loud. Ever.

As Veronica pushed herself against me so that we were shoulder-to-shoulder, I tried not to let out a sigh. *Well,* I thought, *maybe this could be an opportunity to practice my social skills.*

I walked straight into the nearest stall as soon as we entered the restroom. I curled my legs up and hugged my knees, perching my body on top of the toilet seat. I sighed.

"...You okay?" Veronica asked.

"Yeah," I responded. "Just a little worn out. You know how it is."

"Hm," Veronica responded. "You know, Alien Girl, you do have an incredibly human essence to you...all things considered."

"I am human," I responded tiredly. "Just like you. Just...a little different, you know?" *God. Why is everyone so close-minded?*

"Right," Veronica said in a tone that conveyed neither sarcasm nor belief. I watched her feet from underneath the stall's door. Her toes faced my stall the entire time. I found this deeply unnerving.

"So...um, where are you from?" I said awkwardly, still staring at her shoes.

"You wouldn't know," she said curtly. "You wouldn't really care, either." Her dark and smart tone sharply contrasted the shy and feminine one she had used with the billionaire earlier. I recognized her true tone of voice from when we had spoken in the auditorium. She, too, must have known exactly how to manipulate him into favoring her. I was sure that every female employee of his used these tricks of the trade across the board. It was just about how willing they were to let the illusion slip when they were alone with me.

"O-oh," I responded. "Okay."

Then there was silence.

I wanted to break it and talk with her more. Not small talk—I wanted to tell her that I picked up on the tactics that she used with the billionaire. Not in an accusatory way, though. In a way that conveys some kind of solidarity. *I see you,* I would say. *I know what you're doing. It was just as difficult to be a woman in my own world as it is here. I understand.* I thought about what more I would add on to that string of thought. *And I really do want to know where you're from. Tell me all about it. I need a friend. Let's talk more.* I frowned at how desperate that would sound. I thought about how afraid Nancy was of me, too.

I kept the silence until Veronica spoke again.

"Come on," she said. "You've spent enough time in here. Any longer and the boss will get suspicious. Trust me, I've had my fair share of extended bathroom breaks at work, and I would know." Her little quip at the end was quite dry. She did not seem to be interested in entertaining me with it—more so her tone had a vibe as if she were speaking out loud to herself.

I stood up and walked out of the stall. This time, Veronica took my hand. She paused right before we walked out of the door and looked at a device she was holding in her hand. I thought that she might have been checking for some kind of clearance to let me out of the bathroom. *She probably needs verification that the billionaire's still there before she transfers me.* I almost felt flattered, but the disgust I felt with myself quelled that.

After a beat or two, she burst through the door and took off running around the corner of the restrooms.

"What are you—" before I could finish my sentence, I felt something collide into my back. It was a large man wearing all black. That's all I could see from my peripheral vision.

"*Move,*" Veronica hissed. "*Go, right now.* While he's still distracted."

"Who—" I looked to my right and saw that the billionaire was nowhere to be seen. This was the last realization I had before my hands were cuffed behind me and I was shoved into the backseat of a strange vehicle. Before I could comprehend what was happening, we were speeding down the road.

8

DANIEL

I didn't know what to feel. I knew that they didn't have good intentions. I wondered if they were taking me for petty ransom. *No,* I thought, *they seem a little too organized for that. It must be something worse. Some kind of government faction? Rebellion? Are they taking me for a political motive?*

You know how determined people are to get their hands on my alien girl.

I shuddered. Underneath the billionaire's seemingly senseless paranoia, there was true risk after all. My utter lack of knowledge about this world meant that really, I had absolutely no clue what the left and right limits were when it came to their motives. I was entirely sheltered from the geopolitical state of this world, or any other current events, for that matter. What's more, I had no idea what the general public thought of the billionaire. Did they fear him? Like him? Love him, even? Hate him? Were they planning on guillotining him? Did they regard him as if he were a king?

Why? Why? Why?

The fact that there were infinite possibilities as to *why* meant that no conclusions could be drawn. Not even Occam's razor could be applied here; what even constituted a "simple explanation?"

"Make sure she doesn't have anything on her that could be detrimental to the mission," Veronica said. She was sitting in the passenger's seat of the vehicle with a mysterious driver next to her. A barrier isolated me to the backseat. Not that I would have attempted anything, anyway. I was far too afraid and felt far too weak compared to the person sitting next to me.

It was the large man who overpowered me at the amusement park. I could see him more clearly now. His face was oddly gentle, considering he was otherwise such an intimidating man. He was hunched over and looked uncomfortable in the rather small vehicle. This would have been comical, were I not in the situation that I was in.

Without a word, he roughly patted me down. He found nothing. The billionaire would never let me have anything de-structive—I couldn't possess any tools that would be detrimental to *his* mission, either.

Whatever that was.

Veronica turned to the driver. "Is this vehicle blocking all outside signals? Double check it."

"Yes," the driver said after a beat. I still could not even determine the driver's gender, in the least. Their voice was androgynous and hushed to nearly a whisper.

The fact that everyone involved in my kidnapping seemed so very *normal* was strange. I could envision bumping into any of them at the grocery store or on the street or in a bar. Veronica even looked like someone I might have liked to be friends with, in another life. The thought crossed my mind that perhaps I was wrong in their motives with me being malicious. *Maybe they're trying to save me.* I comforted myself with this. The comfort did not last long.

"Restrain her further and blindfold her," Veronica said, this time directed at the man sitting next to me. "We can't have her knowing where we're going."

This was when I began to truly panic. "No," I whispered. "Please don't."

The man, still silent, ignored my pleas and did as Veronica instructed. My hands were bound behind my back and my ankles were clasped together with what felt like zip ties. I was hyper-aware of its head pressing uncomfortably into my wrists. I tried to tug my hands out of its grasp, separating my knees at the same time in hopes that I could snap them off. No luck. I had taken self-defense courses before, but my attempts to use what I had learned in them was proving entirely useless. *The class's purpose must have been to provide a false sense of comfort,* I mused bitterly. *Not to actually protect.*

I began to scream wildly.

"Fuck me," Veronica said. "Would you please get her to be quiet?"

The man next to me finally spoke. "Nobody can hear you," he said. "Stop before we force you to." His tone was firm rather than sadistic. He didn't sound as if he *wanted* to be doing this.

I was unable to process the words coming out of his mouth. I just panicked harder. My body thrashed as if it was a wild animal acting independently of my mind. I could not control it. In between screams, I hyperventilated.

Stupid. Stupid. Stupid. Fucking idiot. Why would you ever think they had good intentions with you? Stupid, stupid girl. Has anyone in this world ever wanted good things for you? Why would they start now?

"Please," I pleaded breathlessly. "Please let me out. Take me back. If it's...if it's money you want, I'm sure he'll pay it. Please," I was crying at that point. I could feel both my face and my voice contorting into something ugly and shrill. "I don't know why you're doing this, but...just take me back. I'll give you anything you want. Let me go." I was surprised by the intense longing I felt to be with the billionaire right then. In a fucked-up way, he made me feel safe from the outside world that I knew so little about.

Like a child with an abusive father.

Veronica hissed, "Make. Her. Stop."

The man next to me tried to touch me. He reached out and brushed his fingers against my arm hesitantly as if he were trying to pet a dog that might bite. I screamed louder and gnashed my teeth. "Stop," I cried. "Don't!" Though I meant for it to sound somewhat like a threat—I was feeding off the mild concern, even fear, that I could sense in the way that he was touching me— my tone betrayed what it really was. A fearful and desperate attempt to get him away. His fingers lingered for a second before he pulled them away and sighed.

I felt shocked. That was the first time anyone had respected a single boundary I'd set since I was transported here. I felt a twinge of sadness at that realization, then a little bit of hope. *Perhaps I can barter with this one,* I thought. *He looks like he could be a father. Maybe he has a daughter, specifically, and maybe that's where a little bit of his hesitance is coming from. I can capitalize off of that. I can use it.*

I could be incredibly manipulative when I wanted to be. I'm ashamed to say that it's a small source of pride.

Before I had the chance to actually put that manipulation into practice, Veronica cut the tension. "Shit," she said urgently. "I think we're being followed."

Everyone in the vehicle was distracted then. The driver sped up, the vehicle's engine roaring and whining. The man next to me forgot about Veronica's command to "make me stop", whatever that meant. I was glad. If I failed in manipulating him, I would not have wanted to find out what "making me stop" would have entailed. Upon hearing that we were being followed, I began screaming at the top of my lungs.

I had worked myself up so much that I began to feel sick. The car ride, now even bumpier than before, was not helping. I still could not fight off my body's urge to hyperventilate. Breathlessly, I opted to scream for help rather than just screaming wordlessly.

"Help! God, help me! Please!" The mixture of panic, desperation, and excitement was making it hard for me to put any force behind my words. My voice was hysterical and exceedingly high-pitched. Nobody in the car paid attention to me. All of their focus was on losing whoever was following us.

The car came to a sudden halt. My body thrusted forward

into my knees. All of the movement and intense emotion got to be too much, and I vomited into my lap.

Everyone was deafeningly silent.

"Did she just--?" I sensed genuine shock in Veronica's voice. I heard an impact and felt the front of the car shift. She cut herself off with a gasp that sounded as if the wind were knocked out of her. Men's voices shouted incomprehensibly from outside the vehicle. The blindfold was snatched from my face, and I was nose-to-nose with a police officer. He did not say anything to me. He merely lifted me out of my seat.

I looked behind me and caught a glance at Veronica and her cohorts. They were all being pushed against the side of the vehicle, their wrists handcuffed behind their backs. In that moment, my vision zoned in on Veronica, and we made brief eye contact. Though it couldn't have been any longer than two seconds, I saw an expression of fear, horror, wonder, and bewilderment on her face. It was burned into my eyes as I was promptly turned around, placed in the back of the police's vehicle, and escorted away.

9

LION'S DEN

The cops took me back to the billionaire's laboratory. I dissociated for the entire duration of the ride back. It was difficult for me to believe that earlier that same day, I was on a date with the billionaire; what's more, I was enjoying it. As I stared down at my hands and tried to make them feel attached to my body, I felt angry with myself for letting my guard down. *Perhaps the kidnapping should serve as a warning,* I thought. *Trusting strangers will always be the wrong answer in this universe. In any universe.* The thought crossed my mind that the billionaire was, too, somewhat of a stranger. He was the most familiar stranger I knew, though.

After all, he knew me better than anybody else possibly could.

The two officers sitting in the front were bantering back and forth as if I was not in the back seat at all. I collected all of the context I needed from their conversation.

One chuckled to himself. "I can't believe they really thought that would work. Three misfit toys orchestratin' a plan to take the Alien Girl? The billionaire's most prized project? Gimme a break."

"They think they have so much power just because they're on the so-called 'inside'," the other officer responded.

I was still soaked in my own vomit, tears, and sweat, but the police didn't seem to notice. The casual way they were treating what had just happened to me angered me. I knew police like this all too well. They were regarding me the same way I was regarded by law enforcement after my parents died. Acting as if they were above the very concept of giving a shit. Acting like there wasn't a catatonic little girl sitting in the back of their car, the bottoms of her little pink shoes still coated with dried blood, as they laughed and joked with one another right in front of her. When the social worker picked me up, he at least stopped by a fast-food joint to get me a milkshake. A milkshake didn't fix dead parents, obviously, and it's not like I could eat it. There were blood-red streaks of strawberry syrup in it that hadn't entirely blended into the ice cream. There was also a bright red candied cherry on top that leaked scarlet juice onto the bed of whipped cream beneath it. This only served in making it especially unappetizing.

But even at my young age, I recognized the look on his face as he handed me the shake that I would later throw away when he wasn't looking. It made me feel seen. Validated, even. The expression on his face was begging me to believe that things would get better someday. Looking back, it reminds me of the look that a real estate agent gives you when he's trying to sell you a shithole, except this was a social worker trying to sell me a shit hand at life. *I know it's a fixer-upper,* his expression told me, *but you can make this into something great.*

I unstuck a few strands of sweat-soaked hair from my forehead in an attempt to distract myself before I thought about that too deeply. I said nothing until we arrived at our destination.

They parked against the curb across from the laboratory. The cop on the passenger's side hoisted himself out of his seat and slammed the door behind him. The billionaire was waiting for me outside of the entrance, fidgeting with the buttons on his shirt. I'd ever seen him so openly nervous in someone else's presence.

"We got your girl," the officer grinned.

"Good," the billionaire responded grimly. My legs felt like jelly as I stepped outside the vehicle. Neither of the police officers thought to help me, so I nearly tripped over myself as I stood up. Looking down, I once again noticed my vomit-soaked pants and suddenly became self-conscious of them. Luckily, he made no attempt to embrace me. Whether he did not want to hug me because he noticed the vomit or for some other reason, I did not know. He silently took my hand and walked me inside.

When we stepped through the door, the billionaire finally spoke. "Are you okay?" His tone sounded oddly cautious and dry.

"Y-yeah," I responded. "I just...want to clean up and go to sleep."

"Do that," he said.

The billionaire had provided me with my own private bathroom, in the least. It was just as white and sterile as my bedroom. It constantly smelled of ammonia. The lights bathed my body in unflattering fluorescent white in a way that made me even more unwilling to look at it than usual. It still felt like someone else's body, and I still felt oddly perverted at the sight of it unclothed. When I entered, I rinsed my face off with cold water. My expression looked unhinged and dark most days due to the lighting in the bathroom, but it looked even more deranged right then. I looked down and noticed that my hands were shaking. *I'm not safe in this world, and I have no other option but to live in it.*

I had no more tears to cry. All of my energy had been sapped. I ran a warm bath, got undressed, and sat on the edge of the tub. Slowly, I found myself slipping down its porcelain coating until I was laying on my side flat on the cold tile floor. The sound of the tub filling up felt distant and comforting, and the smell of the cleaner that the floor had been scrubbed with filled my nostrils. The coldness felt good against my skin. The insides of my wrists were still red from being bound, so I pressed them against the tile. I shut my eyes with a mental reminder that I could not fall asleep until after I had my bath.

I soon realized that I could hear the billionaire's voice traveling down the hallway, but it was muffled by the running bathwater. I peeled myself off the floor and quickly turned off the faucet. I wanted to be able to hear him, but aside from that, the large tub was plenty full, a little too close to overflowing for comfort. I had been resting on the floor for much longer than I thought. I gingerly sat in the hot water and listened to him. He sounded angry, but I still could not make out what he was saying. I could tell from his coldly professional and paternal tone that he must have been speaking to an employee—perhaps a group of them. I could only make out his final sentence.

"You, you, you, you, and you—get out, all of you."

I frowned. *Did he just fire his entire team? Were they all conspiring against him, just like Veronica? Why would they do that to me?*

An alternate explanation struck me just then. *Or maybe the billionaire's just become even more intensely paranoid than before.*

I didn't like either answer. There was silence after that, so I submerged my head underwater. I closed my eyes and blew bubbles out of my nose. I tried to pretend that I did not exist.

--

I lay on my bed, then clean and in fresh clothes. My paranoid numbness had shifted into something like calmness after I finished my bath. The sheets smelled nice and were warm. The billionaire must have had someone wash and dry them while I was in the bathroom. This felt like a good omen. It meant that he was feeling sympathy toward me.

The feeling was similar to when my grandmother would get me a treat when I was sick and had to stay home from school. Sometimes, she would be suspicious and think I was faking (and she was sometimes right), but other times she would stop by the bodega near our house and bring me home a lemon-lime soda and a bag of gummy candy. She would let me eat one gummy after every shot of medicine I had to throw down my throat. When she would walk through the living room door with a plastic bag in hand, it was always a good sign. I liked the feeling of winning her over. I, too, liked the feeling of winning the billionaire over.

I bunched up the comforter and hugged it, nuzzling my face into the sheets. I focused on the blanket single-mindedly. I was too tired to think about my despair and work myself up into a low-grade panic like I usually would. The neurons just wouldn't fire. It was as if I were sedated.

I heard my door open and looked up. The billionaire was quietly staring at me. His gaze did not feel as intense as usual. This time, it had a bit of curiosity and mellowness behind it.

I placidly looked back at him. "Why doesn't anyone here treat me like a person?" I asked frankly. I was taking advantage of his unusually relaxed demeanor to ask questions that I normally wouldn't have had the courage to. Given the context of the question, I hoped that it might even induce more sympathy out of him.

"They don't understand you." He sat on the edge of my bed and put his hand on top of my leg. He rubbed his thumb across the sheet. "And I'm beginning to doubt that they ever will."

He stood up and began to set up the machine. At that point, I had gotten somewhat used to this ritual. I shoved my face back into the comforter and tried to shift my focus back to its texture and smell instead of the uncomfortable feeling of being connected to the device. After a few moments, he spoke again, his tone still dry.

"I've fired all of my staff. Everyone who had access to any secrets of importance are gone."

"I know. I overheard," I responded casually. I didn't want him to think that I had been eavesdropping too intently.

"I should have kept a closer eye on them. I won't rehire anyone. I've realized I need to do this myself." He paused and corrected himself. "*We* need to do this *ourselves.*"

"What are you trying to say?"

ving," he said. "And it's just going to be you and me

placidity was shattered with a pang of fear and disappointment. "What do you mean?"

"We're leaving tomorrow. Rest well and get your things to-gether." With no further elaboration, he stood up and walked out of my room. He shut my door.

I heard it click.

Locked.

It hit me then that he trusted me even less than before.

IO

EDEN

I was dreaming about something that didn't make sense when he woke me up the next morning—I wore glasses, for some reason, and they had broken. I felt annoyed when I was pulled into consciousness. I was still trying to fix them. After my brief pang of half-asleep annoyance subsided, I felt confused. The kind of confusion you feel when you spend the night in an unusual setting, then it feels unfamiliar to you when you wake up. I never did get used to sleeping in my stark white bedroom. My dreams retained all of the color and most of the logic of my old universe. As my brain labored to finish transitioning into full awareness, I wondered when evidence of my old universe would fade away from my dreams, too.

"Come on," the billionaire whispered. "We're going. Just us."

Going? I thought stupidly. *Just us?*

I looked to the center of my room and remembered our

conversation from the night before. My few worldly possessions, only the magnets, perfume, and some toiletries, were in a bag in the middle of the white room. I did not remember putting them there. Either I fell asleep before I got the chance to pack up, leaving the task for an assistant, or I was dissociating as I did it. Either explanation made sense.

I tried to get up, forgetting that the machine was still hooked to my body. It prevented me from moving. *Ugh,* I thought, *my brain really isn't meant to be functioning this early in the morning.*

"Oh! Sorry." The billionaire's tone was jovial in a way that made me feel annoyed. Quickly, but as methodically as ever, he unhooked the machine and whistled a song to himself as he did it. When he was finished, he wrapped its cords around the main body, picked it up with a hearty grunt, and carried it out of my bedroom door. I smirked to myself when he walked out. *Is he trying to impress me with his strength, or something?* It reminded me of the way skinny little prepubescent boys would arm wrestle one another in front of the girls in elementary school, their baby faces contorted with concentration and strain, and I tried not to burst out laughing. I did not entirely feel contempt toward his obvious attempt to impress me. In fact, I found it vaguely endearing.

While he was gone, I got dressed, grabbed my things, sat on my bed, and placed the bag primly on my lap. He returned a few moments later. He gently lifted my hand and kissed the back of it before leading me toward the bedroom door and down the hallway. We had to stay quiet. It felt like I was part of a secret mission. He stopped before we reached the exit. "Got everything?" he whispered. I nodded.

We continued outside. The fresh morning air reminded me of that fateful final night in my own universe. I felt deeply nostalgic and sad, but I tried to keep my face from betraying my feelings. Though his aggressively good mood had been getting on my nerves, I didn't want to soil it by looking too wistful for something that I could no longer have.

It was then that I realized how complaisant I had become. There was nothing I could have done except leave that place with the billionaire, even if I had no clue where we were going or what he truly meant when he told me that it would be "just us." There was nothing I could do to change the fact that he was going to hook me up to the machine every night, possibly forever. And there was nothing I could do about everybody else treating me as if I were less than human. It was in my best interest, I supposed, to just accept my new fate and hope that someday I would feel some semblance of satisfaction with my new life.

There was a small and sleek jet rested on the dewy grass, its bottle-ish nose reminding me of a dolphin. I raised my eyebrows—I expected to travel on the ground, definitely not in a private jet.

The billionaire noticed my expression and laughed. "I'm the richest man alive, don't you remember?" He took a small remote control out of his pocket and pressed a button. The jet's door unfolded and morphed into a small set of stairs. I glanced around as he did this, looking for whoever would be our pilot. Still, there was nobody else. When I came to the realization that the billionaire would be the one controlling the aircraft, I gave him a quizzical expression.

"Don't worry," he said. "I know what I'm doing. This is supposed to be a secret excursion, after all. Are you ready?"

I wasn't. "Yes," I said.

"Then off we go." He glanced over at me and winked. My stomach churned.

I noticed that the billionaire did not pack very many personal items for himself. Rather, he packed an array of documents and personal projects. I did not understand what any of the diagrams meant and didn't know what to make of the odd bits and pieces he brought with him. I was sure that they were of value to *somebody*—what happened at the amusement park proved that the billionaire was within his right to be highly paranoid. I found myself wondering what kinds of secrets he had. Highly sensitive and valuable secrets, I was sure. The immense power that he had from his wealth likely meant that he had connections with the government, in the very least, and maybe even a significant amount of legislative power, as well. I stared at him and wondered who he has exploited. At the same time, I felt a sense of wonder. Maybe even a little bit of admiration.

As we traveled, the sun traveled alongside us, albeit at a much slower pace. *So we're traveling westward,* I thought, and I felt a little bit of mischievous satisfaction. The billionaire didn't divulge where we would be moving at all, but now I had a clue. I knew that once we got there, I would probably have no way to escape, even if I wanted to. Still, I indulged in petty smugness at realizing something that the billionaire would prefer I didn't. I liked it when I was able to exploit his little oversights, even if the information in itself wasn't of much use. It was like solving a puzzle.

I was surprised when I saw that we were approaching the edge of a coast. The ocean was vast and seemed never-ending—the sea and the sky, too, were ever so slightly different, I noticed. It took having my entire field of vision filled with them for me to realize that they just weren't the same; I supposed that the urban skyline of the billionaire's home city, and perhaps the pollution, threw off my color perception. I couldn't quite put my finger on what differed.

"So we're leaving the country?" I asked.

"It's for our safety," the billionaire responded. I asked no more questions. Though he was in a good mood that morning, he was now tight-lipped, pale, a bit high-strung. I was beginning to recognize some major cracks in him. It was as if the morning light was illuminating what was really brewing beneath the even façade he had held since the attempted kidnapping. I did not want to provoke him further—he was getting paranoid, again.

And maybe he's right to be, I thought. I wondered about the legality of what we were doing as we crossed into what must have been international waters. Then again, I had no idea what the laws were in this universe. *And not just the laws humans came up with either,* I thought.

I kept quiet.

"I'm taking us to a small uninhabited island that is miles from the coast of any other territory," he said finally. He turned and looked me in the eyes. His gaze was intense. "I don't think you need to know any more than that." His tone sounded covertly threatening. The smugness I felt earlier evaporated entirely. I resolved that I would make no further attempts to decipher where he was taking us, even if I had no intent of actually *using* that information. If I wanted to survive living with him, I needed to keep my mouth shut and stay unobservant.

He surprised me by wrapping his arm around my shoulders and pulling me into him. He kissed my forehead and rubbed my back but kept his attention on the vast sea ahead of us. I closed my eyes and nuzzled into his chest.

My only option was to decide to love him, so I did.

--

I had long since fallen asleep when we touched down on the island. The bumpy landing forced me awake; the billionaire was far from a perfect pilot. I was just happy that there were no *major* issues with his piloting skills. I knew that even if he had no clue what he was doing, he still would have attempted to fly the jet. He was not going to risk absolutely anybody knowing where we were going. I was worried that his ability to plan and think ahead was deteriorating as his paranoia increased. Perhaps getting away from the rest of the world would help him. Maybe he would even be a little nicer, now.

But to be safe, I told myself, *I'll still be quiet. I won't ask too many questions. Just in case.*

"I've been to this island before," he told me. "It's where I keep the most secret aspects of all my projects."

From what I could see from inside the jet, the island was as unruly and wild as the kind of landscapes you'd see in a children's storybook. The trees were highly concentrated and grew close together, nearly hugging each other in their fight for the tropical sun and providing shade for everything beneath them. Afternoon sunlight dappled through them and illuminated the luscious vegetation that was spread all across the earth. I wondered what kinds of creatures lived on this island. *Maybe I could pass the time by studying them,* I thought. Zoology had always been an interest of mine, but not an interest that I could afford to pursue very deeply. Sometimes I would sit in on classes at the university near my house, but I could never afford to enroll or give up much time to study it.

"I've built a sanctuary here to prepare for the worst," he continued. *The worst?* I thought. *Like when the revolution comes?* I meant it as nothing more than a joke, but when I heard the sentence echo in my brain, I realized that it might not have been.

"You can't avoid the persecution that comes with my status, but I find that I can no longer stand to just sit and take it," he said. My suspicions felt confirmed. Gently, he used his hand to lift my chin, meeting my gaze. "Perhaps my sense of self-preservation was lacking before you came along. But you, my darling," he continued, "have given me a reason to want to protect *both of us*. We will be happy here. I promise."

He pulled me in for a kiss. I kissed him back.

"Let me show you where we'll be staying," he said.

He led me through the thick vegetation. Thankfully, I wore jeans, so I was not too concerned about the possibility of bug bites. I wondered if the machine helped prevent any disease I could potentially catch from bugs—I supposed that if the billionaire was allowing me to stay here so openly, then it was not a concern.

It was a short journey to the building he called "the Sanctuary." It was small, painted with a matte and dull shade of army green, and hidden beneath the giant trees that I was noticing to be rather characteristic of the island. The sudden change in setting gave me mental whiplash. Just that morning, we were living in the urban environment surrounding his large laboratory, populated with hundreds of people. The endless sea of hard grey concrete was replaced with soft green plant matter. No sounds of footsteps or traffic or human voices carried over the clearing.

Here we were now, all alone, for who knows how long.

My face must have conveyed this shock. "I know it's shocking, darling," the billionaire said. "But we just need one another." He pulled me in close to him again. I supposed he was right. After all, he was the only person in the world who could ever understand me.

He treated me more like a person than anyone.

II

MIRIAM

The inside of the Sanctuary looked how I expected it might. It was one large room with scatterings of different projects all across it. It reminded me of a disorganized warehouse. Against one of the walls was a small bed, the sheets on it unmade. One wall had rows of shelves on it with nothing but canned food, so I knew that we did not have to worry about going hungry for a long time. Another housed a whiteboard with multiple sketches messily thumbtacked to it. I frowned at this, thinking about how much more convenient a magnet would have been instead of ruining a perfectly good whiteboard. I was aware that it was an odd thing to focus on. I think that tunneling in on the little details was helping me stay grounded.

The room felt even more bare and soulless than my bedroom in the laboratory. *Like some kind of high-tech bachelor pad,* I thought to myself.

After all of the security measures we had to go through to get inside the Sanctuary, it was comically underwhelming once we actually entered it. A large, thick wall surrounded it. We had to use an access card to get inside. After that, we had to scan our thumbprints to get past a gate to the front door. Then the front door itself had a camera that used a facial recognition program to determine whether we were allowed inside. If it detected a face it did not recognize, it would supposedly alert the billionaire immediately and completely lock down the building. "With this kind of technology," the billionaire said, "Who needs human guards?"

I was unsure if the billionaire kept making such comments to convince *me* that we didn't need anyone else, or if he was attempting to convince *himself.*

I didn't know what to make of most of the half-finished projects inside the Sanctuary. All I could glean from the papers he had posted on his wall was that he was toying with genetic engineering and artificial intelligence. A rather intriguing combination.

"I know it's a fixer-upper," the billionaire joked, "but we can make this place really feel like home."

I frowned. *Am I going to be expected to play housewife?* I put that thought out of my mind. It brought about unsavory images.

"I was thinking about documenting the creatures living on this island," I admitted to him. In my attempt to change the subject, I all but blurted it out.

He scratched his chin and let out a low and amused hum under his breath. He looked like a father deliberating if he should let his child go out with their friends that night.

"Sounds like a great way to pass the time," he finally responded. "Hey, maybe we can even share our findings with one another. Maybe you'll observe something that would be helpful to my own research. Just think of this as a scientific excursion." He gave me a genuine smile. "We're going to be okay, my dear."

I smiled back. The fact that he was allowing me that much freedom, as patronizing as it was, put me in a good mood.

"And there'll be lots of ways we can entertain ourselves," he continued. "We can take in all of the beautiful, unpolluted natural landscape here completely for free."

I had to stop my smile from turning into a sarcastic smirk. *If you don't count the cost of maintaining this place and flying here on a private jet, I suppose…and if you don't count the pollution those things cause, either.* I felt the same smugness from earlier with a newly added dimension of contempt. Guilt immediately followed, then I shook it off and chose affection once more with the reminder that my options were limited. I needed to make the best of my situation. At this point, I had to go with the flow; my new life was far too volatile for me to do anything else.

--

The first few days on the island felt somewhat like a vacation. I was surprised by how much I was enjoying myself. Though I was worried we would run out of things to do quickly, I found that I was coming up with plenty of ways to entertain myself— more than I was able to back in the lab, at least, even when I was still surrounded by other people. My skin even began to darken from all of my outdoor activity. It was dull when we were living in the laboratory. Lifeless. It looked like the skin of a cadaver.

All of the outdoor activity I participated in helped in making me feel less anxious.

I waded in the ocean, found and identified different kinds of edible plants (including a few fruit trees), and, of course, observed wildlife. I gave myself a goal. I was to learn how the ecosystem on this island interacted with itself. The billionaire even gave me a journal and a voice recorder to aid me in my findings. It was true that he was allowing me a surprising amount of freedom, but said "freedom" still had caveats. He gave me explicit instructions on where I could and could not explore. I was okay with this. It seemed to be out of a genuine concern for my safety. Neither of us knew what kinds of dangerous animals could be roaming this island.

Among the first creatures I observed were a plethora of small crabs huddled along the shore. They had orange backs and pearly blue underbellies. I found their colors quite striking. When I first stumbled upon them, they scattered and stared at me quizzically. In response, I calmly sat in the sand, sketched the crabs in my journal, and recorded a brief audio description of them. Though we had no need for extra food yet, I did find myself wondering if they were edible—if they tasted good, even. *Perhaps hunting and fishing could be another way to pass the time,* I thought. *Aside from a way to eat something that didn't come out of a can.* From the way the crabs buried themselves in the sand and hid between rocks, I could tell that I was far from the only creature on this island who was interested in making a meal out of them. My next mission was to figure out what that creature was.

It didn't take long to learn. As I sat in silence and observed the small creatures, I watched a bird swoop from the sky and scoop up one of the unlucky ones unceremoniously. It was a species of heron that I could not identify. It had beady, yellow calculating eyes and all of the physical traits that a heron *should* have, but it still looked a bit off. The birds' coats were dull, and their beaks were not quite the right shape for me to even throw out an educated guess. *They must have evolved differently in this universe,* I thought to myself. *How would I be able to recognize them? All of the knowledge I have on animals comes from my own completely different world.*

This depressed me momentarily, but ultimately motivated me to learn about them even more. Learning about this universe and assimilating to it was the best way for me to get used to my new life, I supposed. The sunshine sedated me. My newfound freedom gave me the will to pursue knowledge, to act like a human being again.

I had not been so at peace for a very long time.

This is only because the billionaire allows it, you know. His good mood is temporary.

You're still not free.

I ignored the voice.

He took me on dates, too. On our third day on the island, he set up a candlelit dinner for the two of us. It wasn't anything too fancy—a couple of paper plates with spaghetti, candles set in the middle of his janky table—but I found it oddly endearing. Though he wasn't the best chef, he certainly knew how to make do with what he had. I told him that I was surprised he was able to do so much with just canned food.

"Well," he responded, "You kind of get good at it when you're all by yourself so often." I sensed a tinge of sadness in his smiling expression. For the very first time, I felt deep sympathy for him.

Wordlessly, I reached my hand across the table and looked at him expectantly. He paused for a moment, as if in shock, then seized the opportunity. He placed his over mine and squeezed it affectionately.

I was still, cognitively, at least, very aware of the kind of man that the billionaire was.

But emotionally, I felt like I had come to an understanding with him.

And foolishly, I started to truly feel that we could have something good.

PARADISE

We made our dates a common occurrence. One night, the billionaire spontaneously decided to take me stargazing. "Pull the blanket off of the bed," he told me excitedly. "Follow me outside."

When we lay down on it together beyond the walls of the Sanctuary, he wrapped his arm around me. I laid my head on his chest and allowed myself to feel comforted. I was beginning to enjoy being close to him, breathing in the scent of his skin, feeling the rise and fall of his chest and listening to his heartbeat. It was not entirely in the usual way that one enjoys cuddling with a man. I think that having my ear pressed to his body, being given the ability to hear the functions within, reminded me of his humanity. That he wasn't an entirely untouchable deity. Rather, he was fully flesh-and-blood. Mortal.

I cannot deny that the inherent comfort of being held by someone was a factor, though.

The stars on the island were brighter than they were at the laboratory, I noticed. *How often did I get to see the stars while we were living in the lab, anyway?*

"You know," I whispered to the billionaire, "the stars are brighter here. The sun, too. And the sea and the sky...I couldn't tell you *how* they look different, but they do."

"It's our differing atmospheres," he responded under his breath. It gave his voice a deep and raspy quality. "The sky is a slightly different color. I believe it's a little more purple here than it is in your original universe, right? I was struck by how your world's sky seemed a little bit...tealish. And the stars and the sun appear brighter for the same reason."

"Yeah," I said. "That's exactly it. The sky here is more indigo than mine."

He glanced down at me. I could tell that I might have said something wrong. "This *is* your sky now, love," the billionaire said. He said it as if he were giving me a gentle reminder. "This sky is more yours than most of the people living on this planet."

I was unsure as to what he meant by that. Maybe that my proximity to him gave me more of a right to this world than anyone else.

I stared at the twinkling constellations with serenity. I was reminded of home. More importantly, I was reminded of the fact that I could never return home, and my heart tightened. Above all else, I was reminded of my final day in my own universe, then I was reminded of my grandmother. When I realized that I had not thought about her in days, my eyes welled up and I felt ashamed. Silently, I began to cry.

He must have felt my tears falling onto his chest. "Honey," he said, "what's the matter?" He put his hand against the back of my head and pulled me further into him. This made me cry harder.

The words spilled out of my mouth before I could stop them. "I want to go home," I said, my speech slightly muffled by his shirt.

"To the lab?"

"No," I responded. I pulled myself upward, forcing him to take his hand off of my head. I looked him in the eyes. "I want to go *home.*"

"There's no way back to the universe you were born in. This *is* your home now," he said. His tone was not unkind. I made my mistake when I failed to take into account that there was still danger bubbling beneath the surface, even with his newfound patience. His danger was constant. It was always within arm's reach. I pushed him further.

"Please. There has to be a way to revive the universe I was living in—recreate its conditions from when I left, or something. *You have to have some kind of record.* Something that would let you recover it, something that would—"

This made him snap. He pushed me off of him. Rage and hurt flashed in his eyes.

"You ungrateful little bitch," he whispered hoarsely. I cried harder as he stalked away from me back to the Sanctuary. I did not follow him. I felt as if this was my fault. As if I had ruined the "good thing" I thought we had going for us.

No. There is no "good thing", there will be no "good thing" unless you find a way to go back home.

Get a fucking grip.

I was afraid to try and return to the Sanctuary with the billionaire there. He probably wouldn't have let me in; and even if he did, did I really want to be there with him?

I spent that night under the stars. I did not sleep for a long time.

Instead, I planned out how I was going to manage reviving my universe entirely on my own.

13

REVELATIONS

I woke up early. The sun was still slowly creeping its way up the sky. The air was chilly, the grass surrounding me was dewy, and my stomach was cramping. I had a massive headache. Oddly, I felt a little bit like I was hung over. When the pain hit me, I turned to my side, groaning and clutching my stomach. I wished I had an extra set of hands to rub my temples with. When I finished rolling my body over, I was nose-to-nose with a giant tortoise.

"Hey," I whispered gently. I desperately wished that I had my journal or my voice recorder on me. Unfortunately, it was in the Sanctuary. *Well,* I thought to myself, *Now I know that there's tortoises on this island. I'm sure I'll be able to find another one later.*

The tortoise blinked at me. I found it odd that he was so unafraid of me, especially after I had woken up groaning and rolling around on the grass. He leaned his head down and slowly tugged some plant matter out of the dirt.

I then realized that I had been sleeping on top of a giant patch of clover. Perhaps this was a favorite spot of the tortoise's, and he wasn't about to let me interrupt his feeding routine. "Sorry, big guy," I whispered. I stood up so he could continue his meal more freely.

I put my hands on my hips and stared downwards at the clover. I thought that this was a rather odd environment for it to grow in. The island was undeniably tropical. I had no idea if the clover grew there because I was in a different universe or if it had been introduced to the island by the billionaire...or maybe someone else, even. I then realized that I didn't really have a solid grasp on *anything* about this ecosystem. I was getting a sense of the local food chain through my observations, sure, but there were still gaps in my knowledge. The combination of flora and fauna living on the island made a little sense systemically, but it was still quite foreign to me. *I am living in an entirely different world,* I thought to myself. *With different languages, different histories, probably entirely different political territories.* It really settled into me then that the entirety of human history as I knew it was moot. So were all the ways I understood animals, plants, and the ecosystems they were a part of. My world diverged from the billionaire's starting from the stone age. The sheer number of things I did not know about this new world was incomprehensible, and I was constantly being forced to reckon with them.

"I have no idea where in the world I could possibly be," I whispered. Saying it out loud to myself made it real. I shuddered.

I had decided the night prior that in order to revive my old universe, I would have to comb through all of the secret projects the billionaire kept on the island. I reasoned that if the billionaire was allowing me to live in the Sanctuary and roam it freely, there couldn't have been anything that I could use against him within its walls. The billionaire was *acting* as if he trusted me, but I knew the truth. He didn't. I only had more freedom on the island because there was nobody else there.

I also didn't think he would be so stupid as to underestimate my intelligence when it came to my ability to interpret potentially sensitive documents; my determination could certainly override whatever lack of knowledge I had regarding all of the jargon-filled diagrams and instructions that lay around the Sanctuary. The billionaire may have been a patronizing chauvinist, but he was not an idiot. I remembered the time he told me not to touch anything at the lab while he was gone. His intense stare of distrust. Whatever sensitive information he didn't want me seeing at the lab was probably not inside of the Sanctuary.

So it's safe to rule out the Sanctuary, for now, I thought. *There has to be more to this island than I've seen so far.*

The billionaire had his own access card to enter the Sanctuary with. I did not. This meant that he was always with me when I was inside of it. Perhaps there was some kind of secret room that I didn't know about inside the Sanctuary...something only he could access?

Or maybe his badge can be used to access more than just the Sanctuary.

Even with the realization that I was always covertly supervised when I was inside the Sanctuary, I decided that I did not want to attempt to return there just yet. Instead, I was going to walk across the island and search for another hidden structure. It struck me that my lack of knowledge about the island's ecosystem could prove in making that mission somewhat dangerous. Although I doubted that there were any predators on the island that would be a threat to humans, it seemed that nearly anything could be possible in my new universe, and I hadn't yet traveled too deeply into the thick jungle surrounding the Sanctuary.

But if the billionaire is able to make the journey to whatever he's hiding, I thought, *so can I.*

I decided I wouldn't explore much beyond the areas I'd already been to. I reasoned that it could be dangerous. I couldn't take a *complete* shot in the dark either, though—I had to play it right. I thought hard about everywhere the billionaire had taken me. He probably wouldn't have led me anywhere too close to a top-secret structure. What about the few areas he *hadn't* allowed me to enter?

I mentally combed through all of them. Some of the places were simply areas with vegetation so thick that it would be impossible to pass, let alone see where I'm going. I wouldn't have wanted to go into those areas, anyway. It was already obvious to me that they wouldn't be worth trekking through, even before the billionaire said anything to me about being banned from exploring them. I doubted he would put a secret location outside of the Sanctuary somewhere like that. From what I could tell, he didn't have the equipment nor the know-how to make it through those kinds of areas, himself.

I crossed those locations off my mental list for then. I decided I would come back to them later if I couldn't find anything else.

I remembered noticing an odd small clearing, a little bit

overgrown, that the billionaire would not allow me to enter. It was behind a wall of bushes and trees, but it was still obvious to me that there was an uncharacteristic emptiness behind the plants. It had the pitiful thinness of a row of items on a grocery store shelf that are all pushed to the front, nothing restocked behind them. If you looked at it straight-on, maybe you couldn't tell...but once you saw it from an angle, it was quite clear that someone was trying to hide the emptiness behind it. When I pointed it out to him, he said that it must have been made by some kind of large predator and told me to keep away from it. Stupidly, I took that at face value and promptly forgot about that interaction. Part of it could have been due to my satisfaction with the newfound freedom the island offered and the unquestioning nature it brought out in me, but most of it probably could have been chalked up to my ignorance. After all, I had very little knowledge on how the different biomes of my new world actually functioned, let alone the specific environment of that island in particular.

As I contemplated the clearing with a more critical eye, I struggled to think of an animal that could have made a space for itself like that one. Though I had much to learn about the island from an ecological perspective, the animals in themselves were not completely alien to me. If the humans of this universe introduced any extraneous predators to the island, I supposed I would have noticed already. The species native to this island would have been long destroyed, if that were the case, but it seemed as if they balanced one another just fine. Crabs were still heavily abundant—if anything, there weren't *enough* predators to control their population. The island's ecosystem was clearly deli-cate. I hadn't observed anything more dangerous than a hawk.

I thought about the tortoise I had seen earlier. Face-to-face with a predator he was not habituated with, he was completely unfazed. It was an incredibly odd reaction that could only be explained if he never had the need to be afraid of something bigger than him before.

Something about the billionaire's explanation was fishy, I realized. That clearing was worth checking out.

I4

FRUIT

When I made it to the clearing, I was sweaty and hungry. I had been keeping a constant eye on the wall surrounding the Sanctuary to be sure that the billionaire wasn't observing me, somehow. It didn't seem like he was. I wasn't even sure if it would be practical; the clearing was too far away from the reach of the Sanctuary's surveillance. Still, it was relatively nearby, and that made me feel anxious.

I was already exhausted from my hike combined with my lack of food and sleep, and just the sight of the thick barrier of vegetation I'd have to cross through made me feel even more tired. I sighed and looped my legs over top of one of the lower-statured trees, hoisting myself up on the branch with a grunt. Carefully, I lowered myself back down. *Dammit*, I thought to myself. *I don't want to have to crawl over the rest of the trees like this.* I realized that if I stayed very close to the ground, I could army crawl underneath the rest of the plants. I frowned at the thought of all of the disease-ridden insects I could attract and the scrapes I would accumulate by doing that, but there didn't seem to be an easier alternative. I got down on my elbows and slowly made my way through the rest of the plants. My hair got caught on a low-hanging branch and I had to stop to untangle it. Aside from that, I made my way through it easily enough. Just as I predicted, I came out the other side with a collection of scrapes and bug bites, but I paid them no mind as I stood up to observe the area.

Luckily, there were no signs that a predator had been living in the clearing. Unluckily, I didn't see any kind of man-made structure.

"Dammit," I whispered.

I got a gut feeling that I should investigate more, regardless. So I did.

I walked around the perimeter of the area and still could not find anything. I investigated the surrounding trees, rubbing my palms on them, hoping I would feel unnatural material to in-vestigate. Still, nothing could be found. I sighed and decided to head back before the billionaire caught me snooping. *He's prob-ably cooled down by now,* I reasoned. *Things will go back to normal soon enough.*

As I made my way across the clearing, I heard a hollow bang when I stepped over a section of grass.

Excitedly, I crouched down by the area I just walked over. I balled my hands up into fists and lifted them over my head. I then threw them on top of the ground. Sure enough, it made that same metallic noise again. I giggled in my eagerness.

Upon close examination, that spot looked ever so slightly different from the rest of the grass surrounding it. It was a little more realistic than the synthetic turf you'd find on a sports field, but not by much. It made a perfect square of yellow-green that slightly contrasted the dusty sage color surrounding it. *An underground chamber of some kind?* I thought to myself.

I could not believe that I had guessed where the billionaire was keeping his secrets on my first try. All it took was breaking away from his influence. I tried to keep myself from laughing over it. *He may be the richest man on earth, but he sure is far from the smartest.*

I traced a finger around the area I had stepped on and found an indentation between where the real earth ended and the metal that backed the artificial grass began. If it were an entrance like I had suspected, it would be just large enough for an average-sized human to fit through. I tried to pry it open with my fingers. It didn't budge.

I stared at it for a moment, dissatisfied. After a few moments, I hoisted myself up and walked to the edge of the clearing. I found a small branch and snapped it off of its tree. In the back of my mind, I doubted that I would be able to successfully use the branch as a crowbar, but I attempted anyway. It popped open with ease.

Just as I hoped, there was hollowness beneath the door. A gust of air came out of it when I managed to pry open the entrance. It smelled of darkness, dust, and smooth mud made from fresh and fertile soil. When I peered into the hole, it was just deep enough for someone to lower themselves into it by hanging off of the edge. I carefully sat on the edge of the entrance, allowing my feet to dangle inside. After that, I reached across the space and grabbed the edge directly opposite to where I was sitting. I did this with exceeding caution. I couldn't risk falling into the hole and hurting myself. It would have been quite the awkward conundrum for the billionaire to find me in, to say the least.

Slowly, I lowered myself into the hole until I was standing underground and facing one of the mud walls inside. It smelled dank, and it was comfortably cool—a very welcome sensation on my sweaty and beaten-up skin. When I turned around, I was expecting to be faced with something grand. I was only met with yet another door. It came as no surprise that the door required badge access to get inside the secret room. I relished in the fact that my initial suspicions were now confirmed—the billionaire's badge would allow me to access this room, no doubt.

Satisfied with what I found, I hoisted myself back up through the entrance. *I'm lucky my new body is so fit,* I thought to myself with amusement. *If I was exploring this place in my old body, I never would have been able to get back out of here.* A tinge of sadness coursed through me with the reminder of my old universe and my old life, but I cleared it away with the excitement I felt from my discovery.

I'll be able to recreate it soon.

I just need to get my hands on that access card.

More energized than ever, I closed up the entrance and eagerly climbed my way out of the clearing. With that, I finally made my way back to the Sanctuary.

--

It was late afternoon when I returned. I waited outside the entrance of the Sanctuary until the billionaire noticed me there.

It felt the same as when I had to wait for my grandmother to come pick me up from school after I acted out and got myself suspended. It wasn't just one incident, either. It happened countless times. It always created a pit of absolute dread at the bottom of my stomach that was dizzying in its magnitude. I hated seeing her sorrowful face. I hated the quiet drives home.

The billionaire, too, was very quiet when he finally walked through the doors. He wordlessly stood to the side and gestured toward the entrance, his face taut in his attempt to appear emotionless. He had calmed down, but he was clearly not over his rage spell from earlier. Maybe the fact that I didn't immediately come running after him after our altercation only made him feel angrier. Maybe he was annoyed, afraid, even, that I had been on my own for so long and managed to get by just fine. I'm sure that the reminder I could survive without him was not pleasant. I'm familiar with the way shitty boyfriends think about things.

Usually, I would find this immensely intimidating. I was struggling to care, that time. My main focus for then was my new discovery and making sure that he suspected nothing. The only issue that his intensity brought was the hypervigilance I knew he would surround me with as a consequence—I would struggle to get anything past him. *I suppose I'll just have to butter him up.*

I obliged his dry gesture. I took extra care to slink my shoulders a bit. I took on the most convincing hangdog expression I could. He followed me quietly through the door. After it closed, I seized the moment before he could get the first word in; I was sure that it would be a list of new "rules" he would refuse to budge on once he spoke them into existence. I needed to beat him to the punch. I whipped around and hugged him with fervor. He stiffened. It was obvious that I caught him off guard.

"I'm so sorry!" I sobbed into his shoulder. "I was so scared out there all by myself. I thought—I-I thought that something might try to—" I let out another fake sob and surprised myself with how high-quality my own acting was. "Might t-try to kill me. I want to stay here with you." Still pressed up against his body, I looked up at him, attempting to make my face look as innocent as possible—all while contorting my body into an especially feminine and somewhat alluring pose. I referenced all of the times I had cried into the mirror as a teenager, trying to make it look beautiful to invisible eyes, to pull it off. I also referenced every time I had tried to seduce someone I knew was bad for me.

It made me feel sick.

"I don't *want* to go back to my old universe," I wailed. "You make me feel safe. I'm so sorry. I want to stay with you forever." I let out some more sobs to stall while I contemplated if the next thing that came out of my mouth would be too much, over-acting, even—of course, I ultimately decided that the situation called for it. "I love you," I finally whispered. I knew that its power would be especially potent, considering I had never said it to him before, but I was concerned that it would be too on-the-nose. It wasn't. I felt his hand gently meet the back of my head. I'd made the correct decision.

The billionaire sounded pleased, but somewhat shocked. "I...I love you too, darling." I tried not to smile at my own success—I needed to maintain a visage of solemn vulnerability. Still, I was highly pleased with myself. I had him entirely convinced. He wrapped his arms around me and hugged me for what felt like hours. When he finally released me, holding my shoulders and looking down at my face, I took it as my cue to look extra doe-eyed. *Like a child,* I thought to myself with revulsion. But I knew that it was the best tactic for his type. I tried to avoid using it up to that point, but I knew by then that it was my only option.

He likes to hunt.

Warped affection was smoldering through his gaze. "C'mon," he finally said. "Let's go inside. You must be hungry."

I nodded. We ate dinner together that night. It wasn't anything as fancy as the spaghetti dinner. Just some canned beans and vegetables. Still, he was back to how he was before he had grown angry with me the night prior. It was as if nothing had happened at all. We played card games together, he told me stories…He joked, laughed, flirted, brushed his fingers against mine. He was happy. More importantly, he had absolutely no idea what I was truly planning.

He seemed to be in the mood, so for good measure, I finally allowed him to have sex with me that night. I integrated this into my plan for a couple of reasons. Aside from my motivation to regain his trust and keep him happy, I needed him to sleep in the same bed as me, and I needed to be unhooked from the machine. He had provided me with my own cot to sleep on; he slept on the messy bed that I noticed when we first arrived at the Sanctuary. This was so I had plenty of space for the clunky machine to do its work while I slept. This also meant that I was unable to roam around freely at night, and it also served as a constant reminder that at the end of the day, the billionaire had all the power.

I was sure that if I fucked him, I could distract him enough so that he forgot he was supposed to hook me up to it. Perhaps his desire to hold me might even deter him from using the machine, if he *did* remember. It would be easy to talk him out of it. There were many things that the billionaire refused to budge on, sure, but I was well-versed in taking advantage of the suggestible mental state men enter right after you sleep with them. *But I want to cuddle with you,* I rehearsed in my head. *Just this one night?*

I was confident that was all it would take, should it come to that in the first place.

He had hinted at the idea of sleeping with me a few times since I first arrived in this universe, but I had swerved him by playing dumb every single time. I was worried that if I rejected his advances in a more overt way, he might have attempted to overpower me. Luckily, he hadn't yet put me in a position where I've had to. I wanted to think that it was because he wasn't that kind of man. Really, though, I couldn't be sure, given all of the other depraved things he'd done.

Before we got into bed together, I took extra care to take the side of the bed that faced the room while he took the wall-facing side. When we finished, he embraced me without question. I could tell that he was on the verge of falling asleep. I prayed that he wouldn't suddenly remember that I was supposed to be hooked up to the machine. Frankly, I didn't want to put any more emotional labor into keeping up my act. He did not. I heard him snoring soon after that, and I knew that I was finally unrestricted, alone, and free to go wherever I wanted.

I carefully pried myself out of his limp arms. Never in my life had I done something so slowly and methodically. Although he seemed to be in a very deep slumber, I could take no risks. He stirred a little bit; my heart stopped for a moment.

He began breathing deeply again. I let out a sigh of relief. Finally, after a few minutes of gentle and methodical movements, I escaped his grasp. As I crept closer to the edge of the bed, the floor became more visible. His clothes were strewn across it. His badge, which he always wore on a lanyard beneath his shirt, was on top of everything else. I had taken his clothes off for him and was sure to not only remove it last, but to throw it somewhere where I could easily find it later.

I delicately began lifting my body off the bed, pushing my hand into it to retain my weight. This prevented its surface from shifting too suddenly. Carefully, slowly, I relieved the pressure off the mattress and swiftly stood up straight by its edge. I stared at the billionaire's serene and satisfied expression. It made me feel a mixture of disgust, rage, and an odd tinge of melancholy and longing. I snatched up the badge, picked up my own clothes off the floor, and light-footedly made my way to the exit.

15

IN A BEGINNING

I wanted to shout with glee so that every single creature on the island and beyond could hear me. I was so close to freedom! True freedom, I mean. Back in my own world, I thought that being able to fall upwards into the night sky was liberation; that reaching out to touch the stars, that looking back at my little town and seeing all of the plastic building-block factory seams in it, was liberation. But the yearning I had to break myself free from my world, and the billionaire's so-called deliverance, was all a ruse.

There was a reason he did not allow me to break the ceiling. It was never about providing me knowledge or a better life or exposing me to "the truth", it was never even about love; for him, it was about having something that he thought would care for him unconditionally. Like when you adopt a puppy because everything else refuses to love you. He was a lonely man. I supposed that in the end, we all want to feel loved, even if we are incapable of truly caring for another being (as the billionaire seemed to be.)

As much as I wanted to scream and cheer, I opted to giggle to myself quietly instead as I dressed myself. I was giddy at the prospect of going back to my old world and finally seeing my grandmother again. During my time in the new universe, I constantly thought about all of the things she had done for me; all of the things I had done *to* her. I loved her. I always loved her. I would never feel a love like the love that I had for her. *When I get back home,* I thought to myself, *I'm going to cook her dinner. I'm going to take care of her. Get a better job; work on getting promoted. Buy her a new oven that doesn't always burn the edges of her pasta bakes. Tell her I love her. Make sure that she knows I really mean it.* This encouraged me in finding a way to revive my universe. At that point, there was no doubt in my mind that I could find a way to do it.

When I finished dressing, I stuffed the lanyard beneath my shirt and sprinted toward the secret chamber. I made sure to wear clothes that were more suitable for traveling through the thicket, this time. I found that jeans and a long-sleeved shirt sufficed plenty in avoiding most of the scratches and bug bites I would have otherwise been subjected to. I did wish, however, that the billionaire had provided me with a sweater that did not expose so much of my chest. That was the one part of my body that was left especially vulnerable.

After I made it to the edge of the clearing, I started running toward the trap door before I had even gotten the chance to finish standing up. I fell down onto my elbows right beside it, taking care not to step on it. I didn't want to cut the silence of the night with such a loud metallic noise. I found the branch I had used to pry open the door. I'd hidden it inside one of the trees' hollows. Just like last time, the door popped open with little effort. I all but jumped into the opening out of pure excitement.

When my feet hit the ground, I whipped around and walked toward the door. I pulled out the stolen badge and pressed it against the sensor. *Please work,* I thought to myself. *Pretty please.* I hated the idea of having to go back to the Sanctuary with my tail between my legs, carefully getting back into bed with the billionaire, having to continue the strange and confusing relationship I had with him indefinitely. It *had* to work.

I heard a click.

The door was unlocked.

My hands quivered as I reached out for the handle. When I grasped it and swung it open, I was met with a dark room. There was a desk pushed against the wall across from me. On it was a keyboard. Above it was a projected image of a login screen. I heard the ever-familiar hum of a whirring computer somewhere, but the thick silence of the insulated underground room was even louder. The room was small—about the size of a large walk-in closet. It was cold. The chill did not feel welcome as it did last time, and the underground hideout felt far more ominous than when I had first found it.

I cautiously walked toward the screen to get a closer look. A message underneath the password entry box read in a small and generic font:

3 ATTEMPTS LEFT.

My heart lurched. I had not anticipated needing to guess a password. I didn't know what would happen if I used all three of my attempts, and I didn't care to find out.

You know you have to try, anyway.

I decided to throw out my best guess first.

Slowly and methodically, I typed it out.

METAWORLD.

I hit enter.

2 ATTEMPTS LEFT.

"Fuck," I whispered. I sat down and thought for a moment. I then threw out my second guess.

PROJECTMETAWORLD.

1 ATTEMPT LEFT.

I placed a fingernail in my mouth and started to gnaw on it. I considered turning around and leaving. I still had the opportunity to return to the Sanctuary and pretend that this never happened.

Then I thought about the billionaire sleeping within its walls. I thought about how the next time he woke up, I might not know what kind of person he would be. I thought about how I was at his mercy, regardless. I thought about my grandmother, more than anything.

I sighed and pulled out my pocket journal. I was glad, in the least, that I had arrived prepared. I began writing.

THESANCTUARY

PALEOLITHIC

I crossed out "PALEOLITHIC." It felt like a reach. I started chewing on my pencil's eraser instead of my fingernail.

THESANCTUARY
~~PALEOLITHIC~~
CREATOR

I began to realize how little I truly knew about the billionaire. I was struggling to think of anything. I didn't even know his favorite color, his favorite food, nothing. Not even the year that he was born. *What year is it in this universe, anyway? Do they even measure time that way?*

THESANCTUARY
~~PALEOLITHIC~~
CREATOR
SANCTUARY
FUCKITYFUCKFUCKFUCKFUCK

I snapped my journal shut. I wasn't getting anywhere. What was I risking by using the last password attempt? I regretted not choosing my first couple of attempts more carefully.

I turned around to leave. Right before I opened the door again, I stopped in my tracks. It came to me. I turned around and excitedly opened up my journal again, scrawling my final answer in large letters across the bottom of the page.

~~THESANCTUARY~~
~~PALEOLITHIC~~

~~CREATOR~~

~~SANCTUARY~~

~~FUCKITYFUCKFUCKFUCKFUCK~~
ALIENGIRL

Hesitantly, I typed my answer into the text box. Before I hit enter, I closed my eyes, fell to my knees, and I prayed. I can't say that I'm much of the religious type, but I needed every possible entity on my side right then. I was sure that whoever was up there could sympathize with my situation. I imagined more of a conventional Protestant god, but it could have been anyone, for all I cared. I just needed *someone*.

Finally, I pressed the enter key.

An array of folders appeared on the screen.

"Yes!" I whisper-shouted. "Thank God, *hell* yes." *So there is a god outside of the billionaire,* I thought to myself with satisfaction. *And it's on my side.*

I read through all of the folders in order, carefully combing through them in an attempt to figure out which one would have the information I needed.

"PROJECTDARWIN", "PROJECTSTONEAGE", "PRO-JECTPOCKETVERSE", and "PROJECTMETAWORLD", they read. Though I recognized Project Metaworld as the experiment that resulted in me coming into existence, I was very curious about what information the other folders contained. *Did he cultivate the conditions to create other pocket universes, too?* I thought. *Perhaps there will be instructions in one of the folders about reviving an "ended" pocket universe.*

I decided that I had plenty of time. I clicked on

PROJECTSTONEAGE first. There was a file inside of it titled "LOG." I navigated to it and found hundreds of journal entries. I scrolled to one at random.

"V 2.4 PERSONAL NOTES: ARTIFICIAL INTELLIGENCE GROWING INCREASINGLY ADVANCED. PLEASED WITH RESULTS. END ENTRY."

So this isn't like the project I came from, I thought. *This must be what the artificial intelligence documents in the Sanctuary were all about.*

I scrolled to a different entry.

"V 4.5 PERSONAL NOTES: EXPERIENCING INSTABILITY IN SIMULATION. MAY BE A RESULT OF CORRUPTION IN THE AI'S CODE. NEED TO INVESTIGATE FURTHER. END ENTRY."

I scrolled to the very end.

"CONCLUSION AND REFLECTION PERSONAL NOTES: THE PROJECT HAS SUNSETTED. THE 'HUMANS' HAVE FINALLY CAUSED THEIR OWN NEAR-EXTINCTION THROUGH NUCLEAR WAR. WOULD NOT LISTEN TO COMMANDS. THE AI SEEMS TO HAVE EVOLVED PAST LISTENING TO MY DIRECTIVE—DOUBLE-EDGED SWORD. ONLY A FEW HUNDRED HUMANS REMAINED, SENDING HUMANITY BACK TO THE STONE AGE ADVANCEMENT-WISE. I AM DEEPLY UNHAPPY WITH THIS RESULT. NO REASON TO CONTINUE THE PROJECT. END ENTRY."

"So your simulation didn't work out," I whispered to myself. "Why keep this so top secret?"

I backed out of the file and navigated to "PROJECTPOCK-

ETVERSE." Just like the last folder, there was a file inside of it titled "LOG." I clicked on it and scrolled straight to the end this time.

"CONCLUSION AND REFLECTION PERSONAL NOTES: THE PROJECT HAS SUNSETTED. I AM UNHAPPY WITH THE RESULTS. HUMANS CAUGHT UP TO MODERN ERA WITH FEW ISSUES—AN ACCOMPLISHMENT. THE IS-SUE CAME FROM OVER-INVOLVEMENT. I MADE THEM AWARE OF ME FROM THE BEGINNING. THEY REVOLTED AND REJECTED ME. I COULD NOT MAKE THEM ACCEPT ME AS THEIR GOD. I FAIL TO UNDERSTAND WHY THEY DO NOT ACCEPT THEIR OWN CREATOR. IT MUST BE AN ERROR OR A FLAW IN THE DEVELOPMENT OF THEIR SOCIOCUTURAL ENVIRONMENT. I WILL NEED TO TRY A DIFFERENT APPROACH. NO REASON TO CONTINUE THE PROJECT. END ENTRY."

Were they...actually sentient? I thought. I shuddered at the idea, but quickly shook off the creepy feeling. Surely, there was no way that man-made artificial intelligence could ever be sentient. It was just a simulation. The fact that the humans in those simu-lations had "free will" was merely an indicator of how advanced the technology was. After all, they were meant to replicate our behavior.

I realized that I was getting too invested in the billion-aire's unrelated projects. Overriding my curiosity, I skipped over "PROJECTDARWIN" and navigated directly to "PROJECT-METAWORLD." This time, I found two folders within it. One was titled "PROJECT" while the other was named "ECLIPTA

KAHN." Struck by the odd name for the folder, I clicked the latter first. Inside of it was another "LOG" file. I opened it.

"ENTRY: SHE LOOKS AS BEAUTIFUL AS EVER. I NEED TO HAVE HER."

I furrowed my brow in confusion. "Eclipta Kahn" sounded like a woman's name, but it certainly wasn't mine. Had he attempted to pull someone else out of my universe before? *Maybe I wasn't the first object of his infatuation.* I began scrolling, only stopping to read what caught my attention.

"ENTRY ONE: I WATCHED HER YESTERDAY. SHE WENT GROCERY SHOPPING. I FOLLOWED HER CAR. SHE DID NOT SEE ME."

"ENTRY FOURTEEN: WATCHING HER GROW UP SO ROUGH MAKES ME WISH I COULD BE IN THERE WITH HER."

"ENTRY TWENTY-SIX: I DIDN'T MEAN TO."

"ENTRY TWENTY-SEVEN: I REALLY DIDN'T MEAN TO."

"ENTRY TWENTY-EIGHT: SOME GOOD CAN COME FROM THIS. I WILL CONTINUE HER LEGACY."

"ENTRY THIRTY-FOUR: FUCK THAT GUY. SERIOUSLY. I KNOW I COULD TREAT HER BETTER. WHO DOES HE THINK HE IS? I HATE MEN LIKE THAT, THINKING THEY CAN TAKE WHATEVER THEY WANT FROM A GIRL JUST BECAUSE SHE'S WEAKER THAN THEM. AND ALL I CAN DO IS SIT HERE AND WATCH WHILE HE MANIP-ULATES HER AND FUCKS WITH HER. OF COURSE THIS GUY WOULD BE CALLED SOME DOUCHEY NAME LIKE 'BRETT.' SHE REALLY NEEDS BETTER TASTE IN MEN."

Confusion did not even begin to describe what I was feeling.

Who was he talking about? What did he *do*? I recognized that his thirty-fourth entry was about an ex I dated a few years prior to my world ending, but I didn't understand all of the others. I could glean, however, that there was a lot of darkness brewing beneath the billionaire's surface. I was beginning to feel light-headed.

"ENTRY FORTY: CADAVER IS PREPARED FOR SUR-GERY."

My heart dropped.

He's killed someone.

He's killed a former object of infatuation. I wondered if I was next. *What the fuck did he do with her body?* My vision was closing in.

"ENTRY FIFTY-TWO: I NEVER EXPECTED TO FALL IN LOVE WITH THE VERY THING THAT HAS FAILED ME SO MANY TIMES BEFORE. I'M READY TO BRING HER HERE WITH ME. WE'LL HAVE A BETTER LIFE TOGETHER.

NO MATTER WHAT ANYONE SAYS, SHE IS REAL TO ME."

I clicked out of the file. I couldn't stomach any more. My head was swirling, and I felt as if I might vomit. Something was wrong. Something was very, very wrong. There was something I had to be missing. There was an extra piece somewhere that I needed to complete the puzzle. The wholesome giddiness I felt earlier had long since dissipated. My focus was no longer on re-constructing my universe. This had quickly become something much, much darker.

There was another folder within the "ECLIPTA KAHN" folder. It was titled "PHOTOS." I opened it.

Within the folder were multiple image files and another folder titled "DAISY BELL." I stopped. Though the folder caught my attention first, the thumbnails of the photos proved to be especially disturbing. They kind of...looked like me? I clicked on the first one.

Now that I could see the image in high quality, I could see that it was *definitely* me. I was carrying an armful of groceries. The photographer was surrounded by a few odd leaves on one side of the photo. It was a little bit blurry. They seemed to be hiding behind a bush, maybe. *But I don't remember this at all,* I thought. A slow realization washed over me. *The billionaire told me that this body was made for me.* I looked down at my hands. *But it's not really mine, is it? Has it belonged to somebody else?*

Who did the billionaire kill to get this body for me?

The sickness that I felt was indescribable. *Don't think about it. Don't think about it. Just don't think about it. Keep your focus on the mission at hand.* I fought off hyperventilation. I could not have a panic attack. Not right then.

Do it for your grandmother. Keep. Fucking. Going.

That thought is what made me push through. When I was calm enough, I shakily pressed my hand over the mouse again, gripping it and forcing my tremors to stabilize.

The rest of the photos in the folder were all similar. They were all shots taken of the woman who inhabited this body before me, who I then realized must be Eclipta, from behind. There were hundreds of them. I did not bother looking any further. I feared that the disgust and fear would be too much.

Stick with the mission. You're okay. You'll be fine.

I finally made my way back to the "DAISY BELL" folder.

Nested into it was another folder. It was simply titled "daisy." *Lowercase this time,* I thought with vague awareness.

That's right. Focus on what's around you. Focus on what's tangible. Don't spiral.

Inside of that was another "daisy" folder.

Click.

"give me your answer do"

Click.

"i'm half crazy"

Click.

"all for the love of you"

Instead of just containing another folder, this one contained more photos, as well.

I stifled a screech.

Though they were small, pixelated blurs of red, I could tell from the thumbnails that they were photos of my body...*Eclipta's* body opened up for surgery. For my own sake, I did not open them in high quality.

Click.

"it wont be a stylish marriage"

Click.

"i cant afford a carriage"

Click.

"but youll look sweet"

Inside this folder were more image files. They were thumbnails of diagrams. I opened one.

In all caps, the title read, "TECHNOBIOLOGICAL INTE-GRATION." It showed a diagram of what looked like the human nervous system at first glance, but upon closer inspection, it was entirely technological. They were not nerves. They were wires of some kind.

I noticed then that the cursor was rapidly quivering. I looked down. My hands were shaking violently.

Click.

"upon the seat"

Click.

"of a bicycle built for two"

Another image was nested inside the folder. It was called "helloworld.jpg." I couldn't make out what it was just from the thumbnail, so I opened it.

It was a photo of my new body lying on the cot I woke up on when I very first arrived. The top of my skull had been sawed off. I recognized the billionaire's hands installing nodes into my—*Eclipta's*—brain. He held a small computer chip between his pointer finger and his thumb. There was a tiny mechanism resting on top of the brain that contained a slot for it. It was then that I realized that I *was* that chip.

I'm one of the billionaire's programs.

My world was simulated. Just like the rest of them. I'm artificial intelligence.

I fell down on my knees and elbows and vomited. Intense vertigo made it impossible for my vision to remain static. I sobbed violently.

Get up. Get up. Get up. Get UP.

I shook my head.

Calm yourself down. Get it together.

"I want him," I whimpered to myself. "I want him." My voice didn't feel like my own through my heavy dissociation, but the feeling was real. I wanted the billionaire by my side right then. It was an inexplicable feeling. When he comforted me in the museum, I felt warm. It made me feel less alone. Right then, I regretted turning against him, going behind his back to find information that I was unable to cope with. I hated that what little good I thought he had in him was now impossible. The information I discovered rendered me utterly and entirely alone in my new world. My one and only companion was a murderer, and I was not a real person.

I wished that I'd never found out.

When my breakdown finally dulled into numbness, as it always does, I shakily stood up and stared at the screen again. Unceremoniously, I closed the photo. I could no longer stand to look at it.

That was when I learned it was a trigger file.

Everything locked down. "UNAUTHORIZED ACCESS," the screen read. Its soft blue glow that had filled the room before was replaced with a threatening firetruck red. I heard the door behind me lock. I could no longer exit. All of the protective numbness I felt drained from my body. I hyperventilated. I felt even more afraid than I did during the attempted kidnapping, during the billionaire's snaps of rage, during past partners' snaps of rage, too. Despite everything I'd been through, I had never felt more terrified in my entire life. Visions of the billionaire murdering me bore into my head. Frantically, I tried typing passwords into the keyboard. I started smashing it at random. All of this was to no avail. It was too late.

The walls in the small room felt as if they were closing in. I hit my fists against the door rapidly, then I attempted to kick it and throw my shoulder against it. I screamed until my throat was hoarse. It finally swung open.

I was face-to-face with the billionaire. He must have been alerted that someone was attempting to break into his secret files. I had no time to be shocked. I had no time to keep panicking. My body was in survival mode. I swept past his side and sprinted toward the opening above. He was caught off guard. He didn't expect me to take action so swiftly. This worked to my advantage. I reached toward the edge of the opening and jumped. Unlike the last time I had hoisted myself back out, I struggled to pull my body above ground. My elbows became wet and irritated from the ground's wetness, but I dug them in further. I could feel the skin on them scoring bloody, breaking apart, shattering like glass. Though I was aware of the damage, the pain didn't register. My panic caused me to flail and desperately attempt to throw my shoulders upward. I felt something grasp my ankle. It was the billionaire's hand.

He was right behind me. Blindly, I kicked my foot wildly and as hard as I could. All I felt was air. I was worried that my flailing and fruitless kicking would send me falling back down the hole. He was holding on with a white-knuckled grip and trying to pull me down. My entire body's weight was resting on my elbows. My instinct was to claw my way across the ground. I didn't dare give into it. It would cause me to slip.

I finally felt my foot meet something. The billionaire yelped and let go of me. The extra support the kick gave me finally thrust my chest over my arms. I frantically pulled both knees above ground and onto the soil. Just like I had when I first discovered his secret chamber, I took off running before I even had the chance to finish standing up.

I sprinted into the thicket. I thought about hiding somewhere among the trees and decided that it was too dangerous. I was positive that he would find me. The thought crossed my mind that he might have some kind of tracking device implanted into my body. Perhaps hiding would be useless, anyway. My only option was to run.

Crawling through the vegetation felt painfully slow. My pulse reverberated throughout my entire body, making my torso feel like a hollow drum. The adrenaline coursing through my veins was begging my body to go faster. I stumbled out the other side covered in scratches, bruises, and a few deep puncture wounds from twigs piercing my skin. I caught brief flashes of them in my peripheral when I got up to run again, but I failed to actually process the damage. Right then, I could not process anything other than my primal need to survive.

My legs carried me to the coast by the Sanctuary. I ran along it and screamed at the top of my lungs, weakly hoping that someone would hear and come help me, somehow. I could hear the billionaire trailing behind me, his heavy-footed sprint sounding closer and more threatening by the second. I snapped back to reality when I glanced behind me and saw him trailing me by just a few yards. We were the only two people on the entire island. Nobody could hear me. There was nowhere to go. *What do I do now?*

The badge.

I glanced downward. Sure enough, the access card I had stolen from the billionaire was still stuffed into my shirt. I thanked God that I hadn't lost it in the struggle. I could escape to the Sanctuary.

I need to keep him out. How do I keep him out? He must have a back-up on him if he managed to open the door to the underground room. I considered turning around and attempting to steal the other badge from him, as well, but very quickly realized what a bad idea that was.

I had no time to think another plan through. I sprinted faster toward the entrance of the Sanctuary. He was trailing further and further behind me. I once again felt grateful that Eclipta's body was so in shape. The billionaire's attraction to women who look like they model fitness gear worked out in my favor. *This can buy me some time to work something more viable out.*

I smacked the badge against the sensor and sprinted through the doors as soon as I arrived. The billionaire sounded closer, now. When I pressed my finger against the sensor, it felt as if it was scanning my thumbprint in slow motion. After it was finished, it let out a jarring error sound. The gate did not open.

"Fuck," I whispered. "No, no, no no no." I wiped my hands against my clothing roughly and tried my other thumb. It occurred to me that the sweat and dirt coating them might have been obstructive. "Work," I whispered. It did. As I ran through the gate, I cursed the few precious seconds that I lost. *Fuck the billionaire and fuck his janky tech,* I thought bitterly.

I faintly heard the badge sensor at the entrance beep. My blood ran cold. *He's caught up.*

Luckily, I had no problems with the facial recognition software. I ran inside and scanned the room for any furniture I could press up against the entrance to buy some more time. The first thing that caught my attention was the cot I had been sleeping on. The machine was right next to it. In an act of strength that I now credit to pure adrenaline, I picked it up with ease and threw it on top of the mattress. I only had a few seconds to act. He was right outside. Only the door separated us.

I was met with the force of the billionaire throwing the door open as soon as I pressed the bed up against it. He was more forceful than I expected. Using the bed as a buffer, I pushed harder. I could tell that soon enough, the billionaire would succeed in overpowering me. Using all of my might, I pressed my hands more firmly into the bedframe and hoped that my adrenaline had not depleted.

But I can only do so much with this human body.

He managed to pry the door a little less than halfway open. I gasped as I felt my feet slide backwards across the floor. Spots flooded my vision, and I became convinced that would be my final night alive. I vaguely recognized that there was blood pouring out of the billionaire's nose. *Did I do that to him when I kicked him?* His eyes burned with passionate rage. They seemed as if they were glaring into the depths of my soul. Viewing his twisted, demonic expression awakened something in me. I felt more will to survive than I ever had before. *I cannot let this bastard murder me and keep living like nothing happened.*

By some act of divine intervention, my body acted independently of my mind. Without thinking, I grabbed the helmet piece from the machine and swung it above my head. In one swift motion, I smashed it squarely in the middle of the billionaire's face. I heard a sickening wet crack. He stumbled backwards and the door slammed shut.

The entire world was dead quiet for a moment. Everything stopped moving. The earth stopped rotating. Then I heard an alarm. A cold and feminine robotic voice echoed throughout the building. It proclaimed, "Intruder alert. Face not recognized." A television in the corner of the room lit up with live footage from the door's camera. It was highly desaturated and staticky, little spots on the screen quivering over the still image.

The billionaire was knocked out cold in front of the door. I had hit him so hard that his face was wounded beyond recognition. Even with the camera's low quality, I could tell that his jaw was twisted. His nose looked completely broken. Blood spilled freely from his mouth and nostrils. It might have been flowing from his ears, too. It was hard to tell.

Gingerly, I moved the bed out of the way and walked outside. I stood next to the billionaire's body. I couldn't believe what I'd just done. I stayed on guard in case he was only pretending to be unconscious. *Fuck,* I thought. *I should have brought a weapon.* That fear exited my body when I looked at his face again. There was no way he *wasn't* unconscious.

Or worse.

I lifted his wrist and pressed two fingers against it. He still had a pulse. I breathed a sigh of relief, but I did not understand why I took solace in the fact that he was still alive; really, I should have been disappointed that he wasn't dead. I didn't care to unpack that feeling right then.

With that, I took his arms and slowly dragged him back out of each entrance. When I finally pulled him in front of the wall surrounding the Sanctuary, I patted him down. I found the badge he used to open the door along with a key ring, his wallet, a USB stick, and a few miscellaneous devices. I shoved them in my pockets and made my way back to the Sanctuary, shooting him a final glance before I walked back through the barricade.

When I entered the building, I made my way straight to the bathroom. I decided that I should examine all of the damage on my *own* body. It was possible that I was seriously hurt without even realizing it. I stripped down and stared at myself in the mirror.

Strangely, I felt pity when I saw all of the scratches and bruises covering my skin, as if the body belonged to someone else. *I suppose it* did *belong to someone else,* I thought. I remembered how my body took action before my mind could catch up. I smiled to myself and looked down at it. "Good work, Eclipta," I whispered. I was aware of how crazy I sounded as the words exited my mouth. I didn't care. I glanced back up at my reflection and met my own gaze. *Eclipta's gaze, once.*

Ever since I first arrived in the billionaire's universe, I tried to avoid looking at my own body. It was a constant site of incongruence, a reminder of who I no longer was and the world I could never return to again. The body still did not feel like mine, but right then, I felt solidarity with it.

My eyes trailed down to my torso. The smile on my face faded just as quickly as it came.

That was the first time I noticed the long-faded stab wound between my breasts.

16

GOLEM

I knew there was no way I was going to get any sleep, possibly for days. The satisfaction I felt from getting the upper hand over the billionaire was painfully temporary. My body slipped out of survival mode and left me with too much baggage to unpack. Now that my mental energy was replenished enough to think about all of the information I discovered in the underground room, my brain was going to attempt to process all of it. Whether I liked it or not.

I sat on the kitchen floor in front of the refrigerator. I suspected that I would hear from the billionaire at any moment. I made sure there were no devices on his person that he could use to get back inside, but I knew that he would attempt to break in, somehow. I mentally combed through all of the ways he could try to make contact with me. There were very few. I remembered that there were security cameras surrounding the wall outside. *I'll have to keep an eye on that footage,* I thought.

There was also a window on the second floor of the Sanctuary that would allow me to see far beyond the wall. I was sure that the billionaire would try to catch my attention if he saw me up there, though. I didn't want to risk seeing him. Even if he couldn't do anything to me, I knew it would be damaging to my psyche. Make him feel emboldened, maybe. I decided to avoid that room.

I considered drinking to quiet the thoughts that were swirling inside my mind. I looked down at my body, felt the same pity for it that I felt earlier, and decided not to. *The least I could do,* I thought, *is respect Eclipta's body.* That brought up memories from when I slept with the billionaire. I winced.

I'm like a parasite, I thought disgustedly. *I'm invading her body. I used her body to...*

I violently shook my head back and forth in an attempt to clear the bad thought.

I did what I had to.

I hope she isn't conscious in this body, somehow.

I sighed. That thought felt silly. She's dead. There was no way she could have been aware of anything that was going on. Any trace of Eclipta left in the body was unconscious. Mere instinct, mere mental devices. Everyone has those. That isn't what makes you a person. It didn't mean that Eclipta was alive in any sense of the word. The body may have been recycled, but it was mine.

But anything is possible. What if she's trapped in her own body, forced to be controlled by somebody else, and you don't even know it? After all, you didn't think you were artificial intelligence, either.

"Shut up," I whispered. I massaged my temples.

Processing the concept that I was artificially manufactured was impossible. I didn't even know where to begin. Though I knew my feelings were real, I also recognized that I had no idea what it's like to exist as anyone else. To exist as a "normal" biological brain. *So how do I know I'm not different from everyone else in this universe...in the* real *world?* What could have possibly made me different? What drew the line between *me* and *them,* what made me *artificial* and made them *real?* I knew that my own thoughts and feelings were real and organic to me, but that was just what I was programmed to think.

If I didn't have a human essence, then what defined "human essence?" What made my microchip so different from a human brain? I frowned. With the new knowledge that I was artificial intelligence, attempting to understand the way an "organic" brain should function was like attempting to envision all of the extra colors a butterfly could see. Studying organic human be-havior, attempting to understand the mechanics of their brains, was possible; but actually knowing how they perceive themselves and the rest of the world was not. You can observe the fact that butterflies have four color-receptor cones, but you will never see that spectrum of color. You will never be equipped with the ability to understand that experience. I could never, ever be one of them. I'm to them as the little crabs I observed on the beach were to me. Nice to look at, different. Novel. But it's understood that I am not them, they are not me, and we will never under-stand what it's like to be one another. Just like those crabs, my pearly beauty could not protect me from being *other* and being objectified. *And this beauty isn't even mine.*

Was that why everyone was treating me so differently? Was it possible that they could sense something in me that was impossible for me to be self-aware of?

I thought about Nancy's fear of me. I thought about the expression on Veronica's face after I had screamed, cried, panicked, vomited. How she looked like she was having a revelation that she could not make sense of. How she looked afraid of me. Both of them looked so afraid of me.

They...they must have known, I thought. *They knew that I was artificial intelligence. They just didn't know how advanced I am.*

I was not special. *He* led me to believe that I was special. But there was a difference between being *special* and being *abnormal.* People fear abnormality. Feel contemptuous toward it. Often find it disgusting and viscerally upsetting. If I was so special, I would have had friends. I would have the ability to socialize. I wouldn't have felt like an exotic animal in a zoo for people to gawk at. All this time, the word *special* was just a euphemism for something else.

My eyes trailed back down to my body. Nancy thought that it was odd that I needed to eat. Veronica's shock seemed to set in the most after I had puked into my lap.

They must have thought that my body is inorganic, too.

The language the billionaire used when he first introduced me to this universe—the real world—was carefully chosen, I then realized. He said he "engineered" my new body for me. His team must have thought that meant my body was an advanced and squishy life-like machine, not true flesh and blood. The billionaire, I also realized, must have instructed his team to keep my artificial intelligence a secret from me. Maybe under the guise of keeping the project from being tainted. Perhaps that was why Veronica treated me the way she did, why I made Nancy so nervous, why my life-like proximity to human behavior unnerved her, why the billionaire fired her when she got too close to revealing the truth...

I felt disgusted. *That bastard's a master manipulator.*

I tried to imagine escaping the island. I would get away from this place, go back to whatever mainland we had come from. "I'm real," I'd tell everyone. "The billionaire made you think that I'm not real, but I'm real. I'm just like you. I have feelings, I have my own independent thoughts. I feel pain. I'm real." Then everyone would accept me, and maybe I could live out a normal life.

It would never happen.

17

NUMBERS

Dawn came and went. Still, there were no signs of the billionaire. I wondered if he was planning something, or if I had knocked him out hard enough that he still was not awake. I peeled myself off of the kitchen floor and mustered up the energy to check the security cameras.

Much like his hidden room, the monitors were tightly packed into a closet in the main area. I frowned when I noticed that none of them had any sign of the billionaire on them, including the camera directly facing where I had placed him the night before. He was awake, but where *was* he?

I told myself to avoid the window on the second story, but I ran upstairs anyway. I decided that all I had to do was leave if he spotted me. *I have the power now,* I assured myself, but it still didn't quite feel true.

I leaned over the edge of the window and peeked into the

distance. It was gorgeous out. I already missed roaming outside, exploring the area, and taking notes on the fauna. My eyes then scanned the vast island more methodically. Though it was harder to see through the trees, I saw a human figure far in the distance. Even from that far away, I could tell he was limping. Luckily, he was staying away for then, but I had my confirmation that the billionaire was still very much alive. He was probably planning something, already. I had to stay a few steps ahead. I went back downstairs.

Something about the new revelations I had to cope with felt like an error. *Anyone* who discovered that they were artificial intelligence all along would also feel some kind of break in their psyche, of course, but the understanding that I was both artificial intelligence and that I was not made to ever *know* that I was artificial intelligence unnerved me deeply. There is some knowledge that humans aren't meant to understand. In my own religious tradition, God and all of the things that He knows are a couple of examples of things that humans can never understand. I knew from my own education that infinity and nothingness, also, are things that humans could never understand, yet we attempt to do so anyway. I also knew from a psychological perspective that there are things humans are not meant to be exposed to, that there are concrete experiences that are far enough beyond human comprehension that the only option is to find a way to cope rather than to face the experience in itself. When the shock wore off, what would I be left with? What categories did my experience with the billionaire fall under? Though he is a lesser god than the one I was familiar with, his status as a *true* human, as *organic,* quite possibly meant that there was a space between me and him that made him inherently more powerful than me. He would know the distance of that space and all that it encapsulates. There was no way for me to understand it. He still had the advantage.

Then how can I stay a few steps ahead?

I bit my nails. I never thought that I would be in the midst of a battle with my own creator. So far, I'd appealed to the creator *I* knew of, the one that could maybe overpower the worldly logic the billionaire used to create my universe. But as I began to understand humanity as more and more inessential, as less and less connected to a concept of a "god" at all, as something that could be replicated using pure logic and mathematics, I found myself losing what little faith I had. I didn't know who created the billionaire, but perhaps it was someone not too different from him. I was tired of being inferior, whether it be to the billionaire or to God or to both or to the humans from this universe. I just wanted to have peace.

As I thought more about this, I fell to the floor again. I crawled into a ball like a child. I cried. The shock was officially wearing off. It was time for me to take all of the damage, psychologically, religiously, scientifically. It didn't matter which one it was. I was still inferior, and I would still experience all of that unbearable existential pain. *It doesn't matter if I'm different from them,* I thought. *They don't think my pain is real, but I know it is. Even if it isn't the same as their pain, I know that it's there. And fuck, it hurts.*

That was the first time I wondered if I should stay alive. There was nowhere for me to keep those feelings. My trauma and my knowledge were overflowing.

--

Rather than killing myself, I existed. Suicide would take too much motivation. For the most part, I stopped living in a more abstract sense. I ate when I needed to, checked the security cameras, and used the bathroom. When my brain tried to bring my dark situation to my awareness, I was numb to it. It was suicide in every way except for the literal sense. My spirit (if you could even consider me a being with a spirit) was deteriorating. The cycle repeated for a length of time I am unable to recall. The only thing that gave my life meaning was, ironically, the billionaire. My one and only goal was to protect myself from him, to observe his behavior, to watch his every move. This grew into an odd obsession with him.

He limped less as the days went by. He was healing a little from his physical injuries, but I could tell that he was physically sick and growing sicker. I wondered what the peak of his desperation would bring, but knew there was absolutely no way he could get inside the walls of the Sanctuary. This somewhat provided comfort. *When he's sick enough,* I thought, *I can leave the Sanctuary and find a way home. That* idea felt too unreal to provide any comfort at all. It seemed as if the entirety of my life would be spent inside the Sanctuary. I could imagine nothing else.

He attempted to find edible plants with little avail. I witnessed him, on multiple occasions, attempt to eat poisonous berries from bushes close to the Sanctuary only to vomit soon after. He seemed unwilling, afraid, even, to venture out further to find the abundant fruit trees I had found on my own. The realization struck me that he had no idea how the ecosystem on this island actually worked. I wanted to find this humorous.

I wanted to feel smug. A strange pang of pity reverberated throughout my body instead. The billionaire was like a scared and confused little boy—I saw the child in him the night he made us spaghetti to eat off of his janky little table, and I saw the child in him every time his rage was thinly masking the deep insecurities underneath. It made me feel somewhat maternal.

For the first time in ages, I decided to communicate with the billionaire. My conscience was telling me that I had a duty to help him, that allowing him to die was wrong. I felt my heart pounding as I approached the window even though I knew that he could not hurt me. My hands shook as I opened it. I could, again, see the billionaire in the distance. He was facing away from me.

"Hey," I shouted. My voice cracked as the word came out. His head whipped around. He looked around wildly to try and figure out where the noise had come from. He was clearly deeply unhinged. His eyes finally settled on the open window and his gaze darkened. He started yelling at me incoherently.

"Shut up," I shouted. "Listen." He did not stop. I waited for a few moments before finally continuing.

"I said *shut the fuck up*," I finally shouted. After a few more moments, he quieted down. I took a deep breath and continued. I stretched my arm out of the window and pointed toward the direction of the fruit trees.

"If you go *that way*," I said, moving my hand to gesture toward the general vicinity of where the fruit trees were most concentrated, "You'll find fruit. Fruit you can eat."

He began shouting at me again. The only phrases I caught in

his wild screaming were "you bitch" and "I don't believe you." I closed the window.

He sat back down with his back facing me. A few hours later, he finally got up and cautiously followed my instructions.

I wondered if I made a grave mistake by aiding in his survival.

18

JOB

That sapped all of the energy out of me. I lay on my cot and felt as if I were rotting.

There was something lurching deep inside my chest. It felt like yearning, and I could not tell what I was yearning for. It was colored with intense melancholy. Did I want the billionaire? With this thought, a new dimension was added to my strange emotion—disgust. But the yearning did not go away. This situation felt somewhat like the explosive arguments I had with past partners that often ended in them self-harming in front of me, threatening to do so, threatening to hurt me, hurting me, hitting me where it hurts, hitting me where it *really* fucking hurts. It always ended with me wanting them. Wanting the person they were when they were not doing those things to me, and wanting, more than that, security. Stability. Feeling like I could have done better and prevented all of this. Like there's something wrong with me, and I needed to be the one to make it right between us.

I remembered the billionaire's angry diary entry about Brett. Brett, for sure, was one of the worst of all of the partners I had in the past. Hearing his name in any context still made my gut turn upside down and my ears rush with blood. The billionaire was not too far off from him, and perhaps that's what made him hate Brett more. As I lay on my cot, I was forced to think of him again for the first time in a long time. The memories were fuzzy, greyish, blotted out in some places. But I could recall the following things with some effort.

At times, Brett would act a bit like a father figure toward me. This could have been exacerbated by the fact that he was old enough to be a young father before I was even old enough to have a learner's permit. He was 20 years old to my 14. Needless to say, my grandmother did not approve of him. When the tension between me and her got too thick, I decided that I would live with him in his dingy apartment. (Of course, my grandmother welcomed me back with open arms when I finally decided to return home a year later.)

During that year, I learned that degradation and control was love. Brett introduced me to bizarre and extreme fetishes of his (which my brain will not allow me to remember in specifics. I accept that those memories are out of bounds.) I had not gone through sex ed yet, so that was my first exposure to anything of a sexual nature at all. I thought that it was normal. My mind developed around that, and I struggled for the rest of my life to regain a sense of normalcy in my sex life. Unfortunately, it seemed as if I just could not make it happen.

He kept a lot of posters of pin-up girls around his room and I made it my goal to try and look something like them. I thought that might make him love me more. I thought, also, it would make him more faithful to me if I were able to "meet his needs." I never witnessed nor proved this unfaithfulness, but I still knew. Sometimes he would come home smelling like girlish perfume, his eyes glazed over and distant. I saw him looking at other girls quite often. Late night walks, late night secret calls. He would share his fantasies about other girls with me, real girls he would interact with at work or his sister's friends or anyone else. I would nod and listen even though it killed me on the inside. I knew that me, short, dark-haired, flat-chested and chunky, would never be able to compete with the older and more beautiful girls that he wanted so badly. But I tried. God, did I try.

The smoking gun was that Brett got me sick on multiple occasions. Nothing that was chronic or permanent, luckily. When he would finally take me to get tested after my pain became too intense to ignore, he would accuse *me* of being unfaithful to *him*. And he would hurt me for it, too. I do have one vivid memory about these interactions—every time they happened, every time he would accuse me of going out and fucking someone else, I would think bitterly to myself, *I don't even like sex. Why would I go looking for it if I don't want it in the first place?*

It got to a point where he made me transfer schools because he thought that I was cheating on him with someone from my classes. He suspected a girl I was good friends with. I can't say that I didn't have somewhat of a crush on her, but I still never tried anything. She was the only person that I felt safe around.

He forced me to convince my grandmother that I was being so severely bullied that I needed to transfer. This is how he got her to sign the paperwork, and I never saw the friends I had before again. I can't even remember my old friend's name. Her face is a vague blur.

I had no sexual desire at the time. It was a chore to me. I thought of it as a duty that I had to perform to be a good girlfriend, just like how I would have dinner on the table for him when he would get home or how I would clean the house when I came home from school, wash and fold his laundry. Just like how explaining away bruises and scars at school was just another chore.

One day, Brett and I had a highly explosive argument that ended in him attempting an overdose induced suicide. I called 911. That was the closest he ever came to dying. He was in the hospital for a week. During that time, I finally decided that I would leave and come back home to my grandmother, recognizing that there was no love in that apartment, only sickness. After a year of having it drilled in my head that she was the enemy, that we had to hide from her, thwart her attempts to make me come home, of rejecting her and telling her that she wasn't my mother and that I had no family, she accepted me again without question. And that's when I knew that the purest and most intense love I would ever have would be the love that my grandmother had for me.

Brett's suicide attempt left him permanently disabled, both physically and mentally. He was put in a group home so he could be cared for while still having a small sense of independence. He would likely spend the rest of his life in that kind of situation.

My grandmother and I moved away from that town, we both blocked his number, and we never heard from him again. We pursued no legal action. I could not retraumatize myself that way, and I knew that the Brett who had hurt me was gone forever. I wish I could say that I never voluntarily got into an abusive relationship again, but it's not true. My next partner, a girl named Abby who was my own age, constantly sent me pictures of the fresh self-harm gashes on her wrists and would burn me with cigarettes. She liked to humiliate me in front of her friends and prevented me from ever having my own, accusing me of cheating if I did. That relationship lasted about four months before she broke up with me when I regained too much of the weight I had lost during my relationship with Brett. Then she ghosted me. It took me too long to recognize that it was still abuse—when I thought about it at the time, I knew that it was better than my relationship with Brett. And that was good enough for me. Then there was another, another, another, to the point that it all blends together. Sometimes I don't even remember who did what specifically. It doesn't matter. They were all the same things with varying intensity.

And they're dark. It's hard to remember how dark my life has been so far now that I'm living in an unrealistic fantasy. But it's still the same abuse as always, isn't it?

Does being artificial intelligence make it less real? It doesn't *feel* less real. Regardless, the billionaire seemed to treat it as if it weren't real trauma that affected a real person. That was part of the struggle of learning that I'm artificial intelligence and that the world I lived in was simulated, as well. All of the pain I went through was invalidated. All of it seemed to be for absolutely nothing, in the end. It was like a really bad joke printed on the inside of a candy wrapper.

Q: Why does God let bad things happen to good people?

A: Because they aren't real.

That entire time that my psyche was being warped permanently, I had no idea that he was watching me, waiting like a drooling dog for me to turn eighteen years old, down to the day, down to the hour. And as much as he claimed to hate Brett, I knew that he must have been thankful for the effect that his abuse had on me. It made me far more vulnerable. That must have been the appeal for him. That I would not fight back. That I might accept him. That unlike Eclipta, I could be manipulated into loving him.

The memories I had felt like a dream. When I opened my eyes again, my pillow felt wet. I realized that I had been crying the entire time. The room's walls were now bruise-purple, and I could hear crickets. It was dusk. I must have been recounting my experiences for hours. A sense of panic swept over me when I realized how long it had been since I checked the cameras, especially since I had been thinking about the billionaire's dangerousness and predation. I got up and stumbled blindly to the closet to watch the live security camera footage.

When I saw him, the sense that he is a dangerous predator melted away. He was sitting on a boulder just outside the walls of the Sanctuary with juice dripping down his chin. Next to him was a pile of the fruit that I had instructed him to find. His eyes were glazed over with concentration as he took another bite out of the orangish-green piece of fruit in his hand. He seemed at peace. That strange maternal feeling returned again.

19

PESTILENCE

The billionaire, though he must've known by then that it was perfectly safe to venture out, was still sticking close by the Sanctuary. I was checking the security cameras for the umpteenth time that week when I realized this. *Good,* I thought. *Right where I can see him.* I frowned and gently bit the tip of my thumb. On second thought, it might not be such a good thing. Maybe he was planning something.

He's powerless. Even if he is making some sort of plan, it will never work.

It felt odd to me to have all of the advantage over him.

Why was he insistent on sticking so close by, anyway?

Even through the low-quality security camera footage, I was able to make out a number of expressions on the billionaire's face. At first, I chalked it up to projection. *Maybe I would just like to think that the billionaire is remorseful,* I thought. *It doesn't make it true.* He began to prove me wrong. The more obsessively I watched the cameras (out of paranoia or out of some kind of twisted care for the billionaire, I still do not know), the more evidence I collected that he was actually experiencing some kind of deep sadness. Sometimes, he would put his head between his knees for hours and stay in that position. Other times, he would curl up in a ball, facing away from the camera. I think that I saw tears sliding down his cheeks a couple of times—he would move his head as he was crying, and the sun would catch the light of his tears perfectly so that they glimmered and flashed. This made the maternal feeling tug even more. It takes an incredibly lonely and misunderstood man to do the things the billionaire did. After all, could he even really comprehend the gravity of his actions? Can a child understand the consequences of pouring water into an anthill without someone to guide them?

Could the billionaire be taught better?

I couldn't say that I truly knew much about the billionaire's background. It was never a topic of conversation between us. That being said, I knew that he must have grown up incredibly sheltered and alienated from the rest of the world. He had plenty of privilege available to him as the richest man alive, of course, but this clearly did not negate all of the issues with socialization and empathy that he was experiencing.

My thought was interrupted when the billionaire began to dry heave. I watched in horror as he fell to the ground, his body convulsing. He clutched his stomach. This had been happening to him a lot lately. Gradually, it seemed that his sickness was getting worse and worse.

He's sick. He's harmless.

He needs help.

I mulled it over. These past few weeks, I had become incredibly, deeply lonely. Every day had been the same. All there was for me to do was sit and question my own existence, question my consciousness, question my own legitimacy, feel hopelessness at the fact that I could never fill the space between myself and humanity. I didn't even know how vast that space was, and I never would be able to in a meaningful way. I would never be a person. I was isolated, condemned to think of myself as a parasite controlling an innocent host's body. There was no way out of this conundrum other than death.

But couldn't I make it better?

I thought of the times the billionaire had made me earnestly giggle. How he was the only real person that loved me, if in his own sick and twisted way, and cared to speak with me as if I was a conscious being. Sure, he was controlling, but it was better than just being an object. He lied to me, but perhaps it was to protect me. I doubted that artificial intelligence such as myself is meant to know that it is in any way "inorganic." There are horrors beyond the comprehension of any being that we are never meant to know. The existential horror of knowing oneself as an inferior and inconsequential speck of dust compared to a greater, unknowable force is something that humans must cope with every single day.

But me, I thought, *I am not a human. I am a machine. I can be repaired like a machine. Made to be happy. Made to cope with what I've learned. Maybe even made to forget that any of this ever happened.*

My heart fluttered a bit when the idea struck me that not only could the billionaire make me forget my old home, but he could make me forget every single bad thing that had happened to me beforehand. I could get a fresh start. I could assimilate. I could be repaired.

And the only person in the entire world who knows how to repair me is getting closer to the brink of death every single day. I'm the only one who can prevent that.

Suicide, though I had been considering it earlier, was no longer an option to me. Death was not something I was prepared to face yet. More than ever, I was afraid of dying, afraid of what would meet me if my life were to end—of course, if there even was anything *to* meet with. Perhaps killing myself would have been more of an option before I was transported to this new universe. I had learned that a god could be cruel, a god could be scary. A higher plane of existence, similarly, will not always accept you just on principle. Cowardice was making living far more attractive than it had been before. I wanted to live. Just not like this.

On top of my own selfish desire to make the pain and depression stop without having to kill myself, I realized that the billionaire's pain in itself was eating me up inside. For some reason, I cared about him. He had been the only person in the whole entire world that accepted me on any level whatsoever. The billionaire tried to give our relationship a small sense of normalcy, but my own trauma and my desire to return home got in the way. My failure to fit in worsened it. If he could fix me, I wanted to be fixed—have a few memories here and there erased forever, be changed so I was a little bit happier, be altered so that I loved this new world I was in. Be updated so I fit into it better. Updated so I could learn to love him.

That man is all I have. That man is my ticket to a normal life.

"Oh, fuck," I whispered to myself. "He *misses me.* That's why he's hanging nearby."

Reasons as to why I should try to reunite with the billionaire kept piling up. I needed to be able to leave the island, he was the only way I could feel normal again, he was sick. However, one overarching reason took precedence over all of the other ones, as much as I refused to admit it to myself. I truly, deeply ached for companionship, and the intimacy he could offer me was the best I was ever going to get.

Heart pounding, I approached the window on the second story again. I thrust it open. Every single reservation and fear I had was disconnected from my body at that point. My isolation was consuming me. What I was doing could have been a result of insanity, a mixture of cabin fever and existential dread.

I cupped my hands around my mouth and shouted. "Hey!" I screamed. The billionaire's head was lowered. He was sitting on the same boulder where he had eaten the fruit I helped him find. He did not look up at me.

Tears welled up in my eyes. My heart felt as if it were being tugged out of my chest. *Oh, fuck,* I thought. *What did I do to him?*

I shouted again, even louder this time. "Hey! Look at me! Please, please look at me!"

Very slowly, he picked his head up. His eyes were glazed over, and his lips were slightly parted. He was half-lidded, which only accentuated the pinkness circling both of his eye sockets. He looked so genuinely in pain. It was clear to me that he really had been crying incessantly.

"I—" I choked on my words. "I love you!" When the sentence

came out, it sounded scarily shrill, echoing harshly inside of my own skull. My voice cracked on every vowel as if lightning was striking the center of each word. I repeated myself. "I love you! I love you so fucking much. And I need you. I want to be better to you, I want to do right by you, you're all…" I had gotten so emotional that the sentence trailed off. I was hyperventilating. The involuntary shrillness returned when I continued. "You're all I *have*." A short, shallow breath punctuated each word, and I was fourteen years old again. "Please, I want to forget all of this. I want you to make me forget. I want a normal life with you, all I want is you by my side, I need you. I know that you can make me forget all of the things I've learned, make me a better girlfriend, a better person. I'm *broken*. Fix me." I broke down in sobs as the billionaire stared at me. He seemed somewhat shocked. He did not respond to me.

After a few seconds of quiet, I continued.

"*Fix me, goddammit!*" I screamed.

His gaze softened. Every single thing on the island seemed to stop moving. Not a sound pervaded the quietness that followed my outburst. For a few seconds that felt like forever, the billionaire and I stared at one another unwaveringly. Finally, I heard his voice for the first time in weeks. Though it was quiet and hoarse, it carried over perfectly across the clearing.

"Okay."

20

FAITH

I felt as if my body was floating when I walked toward the Sanctuary's exit to let the billionaire inside. The bed I had used as a barricade before was still right next to the door. Deciding that it was probably a good idea to remove any reminders of what had happened, I reorganized the room as best as I could. It was dirty. Multiple weeks' worth of filth. I was self-aware of the fact that I was stalling. I did the same exact thing whenever I prepared for a date in my original universe. The excitement of going out with someone never quelled my anxiety.

Additionally, I had to use that time to clean up the Sanctuary and pull myself together again. Clean and tidied space. Tidied emotions. All nice and compartmentalized.

At last, I was ready. I had a realization once I finished tidying the area. As I sat and observed my work with satisfaction, it struck me that it was probably a better idea to give the billionaire some sense of autonomy back. *It could be helpful in smoothing things over in the long run.* That final phrase, *the long run,* clung to the inside of my skull. It was something both unimaginable and comforting to ponder. The billionaire seemed to be far more peaceful now. There was not a doubt in my mind about his promise to fix me. What lay ahead was not predictable, but it provided deep surges of relief.

I walked upstairs. My feet felt heavy in a good way. It had been a long time since I felt such peace. I opened the window on the second story and leaned out of it, feeling the breeze rustle my hair and indulging in the fresh, sweet air. The badge I stole from the billionaire was in my back pocket. Casually, I slipped it out and put it in the palm of my hand. I squeezed around it until four red indents, all perfectly paralleling one another, made themselves present on my skin. As I stared at them, I thought of the magnets that the billionaire had bought for me from the museum's unusually vast gift shop. Even if I didn't particularly *like* the paintings, he noticed my investment in them. The billionaire was incredibly capable of paying attention to my interests and catering to them. Perhaps his attentiveness and thoughtfulness were just, for the most part, untapped. *I could be the one to tap into it, if I were to be fixed.*

I went downstairs and looked at the whiteboard. I put my magnets on it a while ago in response to the thumbtacks violently piercing through it. I took one off. Stared into the woman's vacant expression like it was a mirror. Shoved it in my pocket and returned to the upstairs window.

Day was slowly turning to evening, and the stars were faintly making themselves apparent. My eyes became fixed on them, and my mind wandered to the model of my hometown that he commissioned for me.

I never wanted to see it again.

My thought was interrupted with a moving figure in my peripheral. I glanced down. The billionaire stood silently. He stared at me in a way that almost felt casual.

Without a word, I closed my eyes and took in one final breath of the tropical air. My hand, shaking, hesitant, and balled up in a fist, extended outward. The badge dropped out of it, falling gently onto the grass beneath. I slowly opened my eyes once more and looked down at the billionaire. He had not moved yet. I flashed him a small smile. *I trust you.*

My hands were still shivering ever so slightly whenever I closed the window. I walked downstairs by the front door and waited.

21

ISAAC

The door opened gently when he arrived. I stood up quickly as if I were a child whose strict father had just returned from work. There he was, face to face with me, frozen in place, fingers still brushed against the doorknob. He grinned at me. Sheepishly, I grinned back. Then I felt tears slide down my cheeks. My body buckled. I fell forward. The palms of my hands met the ground and my tears dropped directly onto the floor below.

"Hey, hey. C'mon," he said gently. "What are you crying for?" His tone sounded like what you might use to soothe a spooked horse.

"I'm so sorry," I whispered. The billionaire stepped forward, but made no attempt to provide physical comfort. I supposed that he was still getting used to being in the same room as me again. "I just want to be fixed," I said. "I just want you to fix me.

I can't be good to you like this. I made a mistake. A really, really bad one."

"You were never meant to have access to that information," he agreed sternly.

"I know, I know. I understand why now." *It was as if I opened Pandora's box. Luckily, he can make me forget.*

I continued to sob softly. "I can't live like this," I said.

He sighed. There was an awkward silence that he chose not to fill with reassurance. Perhaps he was still angry. Understandable. Instead, he opted to change the subject.

"Stand up," he said. "Come here. I'm going to help you."

I sniffled and used the back of my hand to brush my tears away. "Help me? Like, fix me? You can do that right now?"

"Yeah," he responded. "I know exactly what I need to do to make that happen."

Before I even thought to ask him to elaborate, I ran toward him and embraced him. I buried my head into the space between his arm and his chest and breathed him in. At that moment, I loved him more deeply than I had ever loved anyone else. *This doesn't have to be the end,* I thought. Before then, I was worried that the only solution to my peril might be killing myself. The chance to restart was the best gift that anyone had ever offered me.

Then I felt his shoulder lift up.

Involuntarily, I jerked backward and met his gaze. My body sensed the intense flash of hatred in his eyes before my mind could. My head caught up with my instinct when I looked upwards and saw the sharpened stone he was holding up high above him. Right as it came down toward me, I stumbled backward and screamed, narrowly dodging the blade.

The billionaire smiled humorlessly. "This," he said dryly, "This is the only thing that could *ever fix a mistake like you.*"

I could not process his words, let alone formulate a response to him. Almost falling on my back, I walked further backwards. It felt like a dream. An awful dream where I could only move in slow motion as an awful monster gained on me. All of the adrenaline in my body screamed for me to move faster, but I struggled to oblige. The shock in my system was too intense.

Maybe part of me *wanted* to die.

Maybe I felt like I deserved it.

Still, my body refused to let my story end there.

He walked slowly toward me as I struggled. He reveled in my fear, soaked in all of its near-palpable intensity. My legs felt like jelly. My arms felt as if they were weighing down my body; I imagined that my hands were dumb bells. The billionaire knew that he could afford to toy with me, and he gladly took the opportunity to do so. In that moment, he had me completely figured out. And he was feeling orgasmic twisted pleasure from his power being literally handed right back to him.

"A failure. An inferior computer with a rotting corpse for a body. My worst work yet. What was I thinking?" The words he spat at me were dripping with resentment, each consonant distinct, sharp, and cutting. Just as I finally caught my balance again, my legs swept up from underneath me. I had walked backwards directly into the cot and fell right on top of it. I tried to get up again, but there was no time. The billionaire was already on top of me. There was no way that I could move. He let out a low and vaguely amused sardonic chuckle. I screeched animalistically as he lifted the blade over his head once more. He launched his makeshift knife toward my chest. Vaguely, I recognized that he was aiming for the precise spot that he had stabbed Eclipta in.

I swear to this day that my body acted completely of its own volition when I dodged the blade. With precision and strength that I knew I could never have the ability to manage on my own, I pulled my body downward. When the sharpened stone came down, it jaggedly hit the top of my shoulder rather than the perfectly centered scar on my sternum. I did not process the pain. Instead, I blindly grabbed at the knife. It was stuck in the mattress, but its blade was still slicing against my shoulder. I felt it dig more deeply into my flesh when I twisted my body to reach it. I paid it no mind.

The blade was sharp. It cut into my hands when I gripped it. Small, vibrant spots of cherry-colored blood spattered across the white floor when I threw it across the room.

Not wanting to give up the vulnerable position he had me in to retrieve his knife, the billionaire resorted to using his hands. My success in dodging his attack and disarming him only added to his fury. He punched me directly in the temple. Sharp pain exploded across the side of my head and a high-pitched noise needled into my eardrum. Every other noise sounded distant. Underwater. For a moment, I was worried that I was going to pass out. I did not. I felt warm liquid drip out of my ear, and I tasted metal. Despite how much I was struggling to keep my own eyes open, I looked right into his. This enraged him further.

Good. It was meant as a challenge. If he was going to kill me,

I wanted our eyes to be locked as he did it. I wanted to at least be afforded that small amount of power over him.

He punched me again, this time in the jaw. A couple of molars popped out of place. The dull pain from his attacks just blended together. *What's one more hit?* If the wind weren't knocked out of me, I might have laughed. I glanced downward.

I became aware of the fact that he, too, had accidentally put himself in a vulnerable position. Right then, he was too wrapped up in his own petty bloodlust to recognize that my knee was right between his legs. He had them spread wide so he could lean over my body more easily. As if it were reflex, my knee collided with his groin using all of the strength in my body. He screamed, partly out of anger and partly out of pain, and collapsed onto the bed next to me.

I used the opportunity to sit on top of him. I grabbed the sides of his head with both my hands and dug my thumbs, fingernails long and sharp from my isolation, into his eyes. It felt like the far more insidious version of a schoolyard bully twisting a smaller boy's arm. *Say uncle,* I thought with vague amusement.

His screams changed into frantic shrieks.

"Get off!" His breathing became more rapid. "*Get off of me!*"

I dug my fingernails in harder. Though I tried not to show any fear, I worried that he'd manage to push me off of him if I didn't find a way to disarm him further. The pressure I was applying to his eyes would surely leave him partially blind, in the least. The pain he was feeling in his lower body would fade soon, however, leaving his full strength at his disposal again. My new body was strong, but the billionaire was still somewhat of an even match. I had to think of a solution quickly.

Before I could finish mulling over a plan, he loudly and desperately interrupted me.

"Eclipta! Please!"

I looked down at him. A mixture of abhorrence and quiet fury pulsed through my body.

"I'm not Eclipta," I whispered coldly. "My name is Daisy."

I then realized that the pillow at the end of the cot was within arm's reach. Without second thought, I grabbed it and pressed it into his face. He continued to scream.

"Shut...the...fuck...up," I panted. "Go...to...sleep. You fucking...*bastard.*"

His muffled shrieks devolved into the sobs of a panicked little boy. Though the pillow muffled his speech, I could perfectly understand the last few words that exited his mouth.

"Eclipta, stop! Please!"

I stared intensely into the pillow as he took his final shallow breaths, ignoring the wrong name he was calling me in his fear-induced delirium. Having learned by that point that the billionaire is an especially good actor, I continued to press the pillow into his face with all of my strength long after he stopped moving. His body turned pale. Eventually, I cautiously lifted one hand from the pillow to press two fingers against his wrist.

No pulse.

Flesh and blood mortal, he was.

Over the course of what must have been merely a twenty-minute-long struggle, I had gone from loving the billionaire in all of his abusive madness to becoming his murderer. Some kind of fear and disgust stopped me from lifting the pillow from his head. The feelings were vague, somewhat directed at myself and somewhat directed at my victim.

Victim.

He had been struggling with such intensity that all of the dampness from his face leaked through the flat, old pillow. I could feel it beneath my hands. A mixture of sweat, tears, snot, maybe a little bit of blood that I could not see yet. In fact, I decided that I never wanted to see it.

So, I never did lift that pillow up. Looking at his dead face would anguish me too much. It might have made me cry. He was the last person on earth that I ever wanted to cry over. Even after his death, I refused to commit such an action that would have been so satisfying to him.

I was in a trance when I shakily lifted myself from his body. I did it gently, as if he were just sleeping, as if he would still be able to feel it if I put too much of my weight on his chest. *Easy does it, one shaky leg after the other. Now stand.* Of course, he could not feel it. He never would again.

I walked out of the door of the Sanctuary covered in blood and viscera. I became aware of the fact that we all come into the world covered in viscera, then we often leave it in the same way. I found it profound that both times, we are covered in reminders that we are flesh. That after everything, we are merely another animal among many on this planet. Marked with evidence of our birth, then evidence of our death. Returning to the depths of the unknown. Returning to that structureless and timeless plane of endless sensation, no sensation. Retreating from all of the embarrassment that this world has conditioned us to feel and has forced us to endure every time there is a reminder that we have the same desires as every other creature on this planet—to eat copiously, hoard, pleasure ourselves, copulate, indulge, avoid pain, avoid discomfort, use the energy life has given us selfishly. Survive. Nancy was wrong. Flesh is beautiful.

I realized then that I was a virgin birth, technically. I laughed loudly over this. I felt incredibly enlightened to something. I cannot tell you what that something is. It is unable to be articulated.

I picked a direction. *Any of them will do,* I thought. After all, I was living on an island. It all led to the same coast, shaped like an ouroboros. As above, so below. Better luck next time.

Many isolated peoples have a different concept of time or direction than the rest of the world. Most of these societies exist on islands. As someone who was also isolated not only from the rest of the world, but from any other living human being at all, I decided that I no longer needed to consider things like time, direction, or space at all. So, I just walked. To somewhere, over some amount of time. No more specifics. I knew that things would fall into place. My fate would guide me.

And it did. I came across a cliff, eventually. It was tall and green, looking as if it were reaching nice and high for the bright moon above. A group of the little pearl-bellied crabs I had been studying during my time there were congregated together at the top. Though I try not to project human qualities onto animals, I could not help but notice that the crabs were staring up at the stars above them, and I wondered if they found any beauty in the night sky. It was entirely possible. Anything in this universe was possible, it seemed. It's why I hated living in it.

The island always had a perfectly clear atmosphere. Untouched by pollution of any kind and hardly ever overcast. In my day-to-day life, it was rare for me to get the opportunity to look up at the stars. It was rare for me to look anywhere except at what was below, in fact. My neck was at a permanent down-facing angle. I didn't have time to appreciate the beauty in the sky. I needed to watch out for whatever was on the ground. Yet there I was, observing those little twinkles of light with the crabs.

Wondrously, they were completely undisturbed by my presence. They made no attempt to scatter down the cliff whenever I approached the top of it. Perhaps they had gotten used to me and began to trust me as I peacefully observed their behavior. The crabs may have noticed by then that I was not like one of the hawks patrolling the sky for a meal. Or maybe, like me, they had absolutely no sense of self-preservation. Or maybe, after all this time, I really was a hawk all along.

Their bright orange backs contrasted with their pretty bluish underbellies made them prime targets to anything watching them from above. I, too, must have had some kind of target on my back. A target that I was unaware of and was impossible to change, in any case. It could have been mental illness. The way I differed from people in my new universe. The way I differed from people in my home universe, too. My trauma. My predisposition to let the wrong people in. The cycle I was stuck in. It didn't matter. It was there. Ouroboros. The universe experiencing itself. The universe eating itself. Hawk eat little crab eat hawk.

When I reached the very top of the cliff, I did not sit down. I stood with my hands clasped behind my back and placidly stared upward.

My eyes closed softly. I breathed in the night air, savored it in my lungs. Slowly let it back out of my nostrils. Rinse and re-peat. When my eyes opened again, they were fixed on the ocean beneath the cliff.

There is a way out.

How did you transport yourself here in the first place, Daisy?

I smiled a little bit. *If there's a God,* I thought, *and if they are merciful...they will save me. They will take me somewhere else. Give me a fresh start in a brand-new world, just like* he *did.*

The other half of my internal conversation challenged this. *And if there's not? And if they aren't?*

Though I continued smiling, it took on a sadder flavor. *Then this is still an escape.*

With no further input from me, my conscience, my internal debate, nor my body, I slowly walked backwards. The crabs parted to make way for me, but they still did not scatter. Not until I took off running.

Then I tried to touch the stars.

EPILOGUE

"Give me your 20, Xanthippe."

Veronica hesitated before replying. She sighed, pressed the button on her device, and spoke into it. "Code?" *They forget. Every. Damn. Time.*

"Darwin." Even through the low-quality and staticky audio, Veronica sensed annoyance in her conversation partner's tone. Her cohorts were well aware that the communication devices Veronica had built for their missions were highly protected from outside interference, near impenetrable. They viewed her insistence on extra authentication as either tedious or evidence that she did not have faith in her own creations. She didn't care. She knew that it was *always* better to be cautious. That was why she was in the position she was in, and *they* held the positions that *they* were in.

Though they did not ask for it, Veronica passive-aggressively gave the proper callback to the code word. "*Archipelago.* Zero degrees seven minutes south over ninety degrees fifty-nine minutes west. Over."

There was a pause. "10-9. Over."

Veronica wanted to tear her hair out. She spoke more slowly (and admittedly, condescendingly) the second time. "Pay attention. Zero seven south, ninety fifty-nine west. Eyes on location, preparing for landing. Over."

Another pause. "Roger, Xanthippe. Over and out."

Despite the irritation she felt with the incompetence of her partners, Veronica was in a rather cheerful mood. She was very pleased, excited, even, with the org's success in locating the billionaire's secret island. He had been missing for months. She was positive that he was still there, somewhere. Dead, likely. The *likely* warped her excitement into anxiety, as if it brought the possibility that he could be anything else. Still, the evidence was clear. Veronica had long since injected a tracking device into the billionaire while he slept, and he had remained motionless for days. She highly doubted that he somehow found out about the device and tampered with it. It was nearly undetectable. That didn't mean there wasn't a chance.

Either way, she felt as if she had tossed her inclination to be overly cautious out the window in going on the mission alone. After her cohorts had put their recklessness and ignorance on full display—*showed their entire asses,* as Veronica had lectured them—she was not going to risk taking anyone else along with her. They were caught before they ever got started when they attempted to steal the billionaire's Alien Girl project. Her get-away driver had failed in actually blocking any outside signal. Miserably. The memory still made her angry when she thought about it. It almost ruined their entire mission. Luckily, the billionaire chose not to press charges against any of them. Though she was not sure why he did that at the time—definitely not out of the *goodness of his heart,* that was for sure—she now had her suspicions. Perhaps he was in a highly gray legal area himself, to say the least. This mission would help her in confirming them.

Her landing was unusually smooth. This pleased her. Her flight training was paying off. When she stepped out of her aircraft, the usual nausea and jelly-leg feeling was not present. She stretched her arms high above her head before putting her hands on her hips and surveying the surrounding area. *Very peaceful.*

When she noticed the Sanctuary in the distance, she smiled with satisfaction. "One of these things is not like the others," she muttered in a sing-song tone.

It was heavily guarded. Veronica anticipated that it might be, and she came greatly prepared. The one thing that the billionaire was never able to surpass her in was her ability to hack whatever dumbass technology he tried to create without her help. His access control systems were low-frequency and heavily antiquated. *Stupidly easy to crack. He probably built it using some open-source bullshit.*

She was correct. Very correct. She never even got the chance to emulate his access card, but her device still worked its magic on the card reader using one of the default keys she had downloaded from the internet. *Right on the money. Open-source bullshit,* she thought.

After she entered its first set of walls, she slid right past the fingerprint reader with ease. It was the same situation as before. The billionaire had used open-source technology that Veronica already knew how to exploit like the back of her hand. It only took using one of her many tools to gain access. "Go-go gadget master print," she muttered as she pulled something out of her bag. It was a synthetic fingerprint. It had all of the basic traits of a print that every human being possessed. If the scanner was rudimentary enough, it would accept the scan—and sure enough, it did.

Before she continued onward, she had already noticed the camera by the front door. She sat down where it could not detect her. She knew that the billionaire had a thing for booby traps, particularly at the very end of whatever security system he had created. Humming, she opened up her backpack and pulled out a set of face paints. *Maybe I won't even need them,* she thought, chuckling to herself with dry amusement. She was reminded of a scandal the billionaire was subject to years ago over his tech being racially biased. A piece of facial recognition software he had single-handedly developed failed to detect Black faces. It also had difficulty recognizing women. All of the subjects that he tested it on and developed it around were white, most of them gender-conforming men. This was especially dense of the billionaire when you considered the fact that there was an abundance of women who worked alongside him. In fact, Veronica worked with him the most out of anyone else—yet his software, sure enough, failed to detect her dark skin.

Feels oddly symbolic, she mused.

That scandal must have been the point where the last lingering thread of Veronica's faith in the billionaire's intelligence was broken. Despite what the public thought, he was not rich because he was *smart.* He had simply always been spoiled and self-centered. Why would he consider anyone who was not a white cis man? After all, *he* was a white cis man, and *he* was all that mattered. *The sun rises and sets out of his ass. Just ask him.* Veronica grinned at her crude joke.

She took out a tube of hot pink paint. She spread it all over her face, also applying it to her arms and legs for good measure. She smeared it all around as if it were sunscreen. That would be her base color.

Next, she used navy blue paint to draw geometric lines across her forehead, her hands, her forearms; anywhere that skin was visible. She did the same with neon green paint, then bright orange. Any color that was not a natural skin tone was fair game.

When she finally felt confident enough, she swept a piece of cloth over her head, tied it underneath her chin, and approached the security camera. Nothing happened. Good. And bad. She still needed the door to open.

She sighed and ruffled her hands in her bag again. She'd hoped she wouldn't have to use such a ridiculous method, but it was obvious now that it was necessary.

She held a low-quality, hastily printed-out picture of the billionaire's face up to the camera. Admittedly, she chose an especially unflattering picture of him mid-speech. It was a meme for a while.

The doors opened.

Veronica howled with laughter. "God, his technology fucking sucks!"

Her cavalier attitude dissipated as soon as she entered the room. She froze. Though she expected to be met with the billionaire's corpse, she wasn't quite prepared to behold such a gruesome sight. Everything in the room was messy, covered in blood, broken, or all three. The billionaire, like a morbid centerpiece, lay in the center of it all on top of a cot. A pillow—now dry, but with a mysterious pink stain exploding from its center—rested on top of his head. She tried not to vomit when the smell hit her. It was disgustingly sweet, metallic, and pungent with overbearing rot. Weirdly, she was reminded of when girls in middle school tried to hide the pubescent intensity of body odor lingering around them with cheap fruity-smelling body spray. Both smells felt like a poor attempt at disguise.

She covered her nose with her shirt and pulled a camera

out of her bag. She took photos of everything in the room with great caution. When she hesitantly leaned over the billionaire to take a photo of his cadaver, she caught another odor. This time, it smelled like bad breath. Not just bad, actually. *Awful.* She thought about the fact that his open mouth must be what lay beneath the pillow, his saliva laying stagnant inside of it like a sick primordial soup. She felt as if she might throw up again. She quickly pushed that image out of her mind.

No other human had ever existed on this island with him. Only one person could be his murderer.

She bit her lip, enraptured in deep thought. *Alien Girl. Did she turn evil?*

She pondered it for a moment, then she smirked. *Nah. Nobody, evil machine or not, could put up with the billionaire's shit for very long.*

The word "machine" felt wrong, for some reason. She shuddered uncomfortably.

After taking a photo of the billionaire, she approached a large white machine, all of its pieces scattered across the floor. She recognized it as Alien Girl's charging device. She knew that the billionaire undressed her and hooked her up to it every night before she would go into sleep mode. Countless electrodes dangled off of it. Further away from the machine was a thin helmet. It used to be attached to the machine with a wire, but it was now broken away. Upon closer inspection, the helmet was speckled with dried blood.

Veronica frowned at this. She had deep suspicions about Alien Girl ever since she threw up in the back of the vehicle. It would not be uncharacteristic of the billionaire to pay odd attention to detail in producing Alien Girl's likeness to a real human—after all, her body was strangely realistic, and she got the impression that he wanted an especially life-like sex doll—but Veronica was starting to think that she was not really an android. A silly thought, she knew, but there was only one way to alleviate it.

She opened her bag and took out a screwdriver. Carefully, she used it to twist every screw she could find out of place. There were only four on the entire machine, securing a single panel on top of it. *Strange,* she thought. *You'd think there would be more points of access to its innards.*

Her fingernails delicately traced around the perimeter of the panel. When she managed to get them between its cracks, she used them to lift it up with precision.

She looked inside.

Hollow.

Nothing.

The only thing inside of it was a power supply to the indicator light. She now knew that it wasn't an "indicator" light at all. There was nothing *to* indicate. The machine was just a decoy.

Veronica blinked rapidly, slack jawed. She looked again to make sure her eyes were not deceiving her. They weren't.

She picked up the machine and smashed it against the floor. With an uncharacteristic lack of regard for how useful it would be as evidence, she kicked it repeatedly, ignoring the pain she felt in her foot every time it collided with the hard metal material.

"Pervert. Pervert!" she spat through gritted teeth.

When she was done, the machine was still intact, but its perfect gleaming finish was ruined. Numerous scuffs peppered its surface. She frowned deeply, feeling her eyes become glossier, and put her hand up to her mouth. She thought of her own history with the billionaire. How they went to the same university, enrolled in the same program, her opportunity of a lifetime—her, twelve years old, and him, nineteen, begrudgingly attending out of family obligation. Him, a perfect specimen of what nepotism does for a child. Her, the opposite. *Lottery winner,* he'd called her derisively. The rivalry, then the friendship. The partnership.

His proposition on her eighteenth birthday. The punishment for rejection-- demotion. "Can't work on the same level with that tension there," he said. The further punishment if she were to ever dare leave his company for something better. The fucking patron saint of blacklisting.

She took deep breaths and became calm and level again. Without taking her eyes off the machine, she picked up her transmission device. "Whiskey, code word Darwin," she stated with newfound equanimity.

"Archipelago. Talk to me, Xanthippe."

"Subject has been located. 10-45D. As suspected. Over."

"Copy. Is assistance necessary? Over."

"Negative, but stay ready. Over and out."

She lowered her transmission device again and stared at the machine. There was absolutely no way that Alien Girl had an inorganic body. She had to have a power source for that to be possible, and the one thing that could have provided that was merely a chromatic husk. This proved to Veronica above all else that Alien Girl's body was all-natural.

"But where did it come from?" she whispered.

Her next task was to find Alien Girl, dead or alive. She had a feeling that she had only just begun unraveling a string of dark secrets.

She finished examining the rest of the Sanctuary. Still no sign of her. *We might have a runaway situation on our hands.*

When Veronica stepped outside again, she noticed a clearing nearby that was guarded behind a thin thicket. According to her prior research, this island didn't have any animals living on it that could make a clearing like that.

Except for a human. Someone has been trying to hide something.

With difficulty, she climbed through it. "God," she whispered, chuckling under her breath as she labored to make it through the other side. "Why have you always been so shit at taking proper security measures?" Veronica always liked the feeling of getting one over on the billionaire. It was so easy, yet so rewarding.

When she stumbled through the last of the plants, she could not see anything of importance. Just grass.

"I know you're hiding something," she muttered. "There has to be *something*."

She put her hands on her hips and walked around the perimeter of the clearing with sharp-eyed intent. Absolutely nothing.

Finally, she decided to walk through the center of it. She paced back and forth, staring into the ground intensely. Then her feet fell from underneath her.

Veronica screamed. Just like that, she fell through the ground. Like it was second nature, she positioned herself so she fell on whatever lay beneath her in a favorable position. She always had decent reflexes. They definitely came in handy, this time.

When she opened her eyes, she saw that she was in a muddy hole. It was completely dark save for the sunshine filtering in from directly above her. A square metal door rested directly beneath her body. When she looked up above her, she noticed that the hole in the ground was roughly the same size as the door. It must have been poorly engineered. She was surprised that the door was able to support itself for that long in the muddy ground. "Moron," she muttered. She stood up and dusted herself off.

As she stood up, she noticed another door directly in front of her. It, too, required an access card.

"Jesus Christ, dude," she said. "I've played children's RPGs harder than this." She laughed at her own joke as she whipped out her card reading device. She smirked with satisfaction when she heard the door click open.

When she entered the room, she was put off by the red screen that met her. It declared that all of the files on the computer had been encrypted due to unauthorized access. Someone had tried to get into something they were not supposed to. This did not deter her, though. Luckily, she easily recognized the operating system on the computer. It was proprietary to the company. She led the security aspect of its development long after she had secretly begun organizing with other company members. She remembered how giddy she felt when she secretly developed a piece of decryption software alongside the OS's built in security system. It opened up endless opportunities to slowly leak information to the public. And now, it opened up an opportunity for her to access all of the files that she needed to.

Only Veronica had access to the decryption software. She kept it in an inconspicuous looking thumb drive in her backpack. It was shaped like a little kitty—the flash drive's connector plug became visible when you pulled off its head. She pulled out the thumb drive and inserted it into the computer. It automatically launched the software. The computer's fan whirred laboriously and unsteadily. When the program finally opened, it settled into a quiet hum.

Veronica, too, hummed under her breath as she clicked the "run process" button on the software's home page. After about thirty minutes of waiting (impatiently, she had to admit), the encryption process was entirely reversed. It was as if the computer had never gone into lockdown mode at all. But what triggered it in the first place?

Before going through anything, she prompted the software to check for any unusual triggers in the computer's files. Only a photo titled "helloworld.jpg" appeared under the "suspicious files" category. She scrolled through its data and found that automatic encryption would be triggered if the file were closed improperly. *I guess I'll take a look at that file last, copy everything over to an external drive, and close it using a command prompt.*

An amused grin spread over her face. *Man. It would be hilarious if all I could find on this computer was some weird porn, or something.* Just as quickly as the smirk arrived, it fell from her expression. She knew that whatever she found would likely be worse than that. Far worse. She couldn't try to keep herself amused anymore. The situation was too serious. She had learned too many unsavory facts about the billionaire to find any more genuine humor in his pathetic and perverted nature. Veronica was very aware that he was an awful person. She and the billionaire went way back, yet he still managed to keep surprising her in the worst of ways.

She placed a hand over her chest and breathed in deeply, feeling it rise and fall beneath her palm. This helped her in grounding herself before she got to work. Most of the folder names were easily recognizable. Veronica didn't feel very interested in reading through the billionaire's earlier projects right then. Her initiative was to discover information that was related to Alien Girl-- what Alien Girl was *truly* composed of. The billionaire had been lying. There were likely far more secrets beneath the underbelly of Project Metaworld. So, she navigated to the folder titled "PROJECTMETAWORLD" first. "Nice and blatant file names," she muttered sarcastically. Though she thought it was stupid of him to make his folder titles so obvious, she was, of course, grateful for such stupidity.

Two more folders were nested inside. One was titled "PROJECT." The other was titled "ECLIPTA KAHN." Veronica quirked an eyebrow upon viewing the latter. "Who the hell is Eclipta?" she whispered to herself. She quickly navigated to the folder. Inside of it was a text file. It was difficult for Veronica to avoid the temptation to read every single thing within it, so she scrolled through it quickly, stopping where she caught interesting bits and pieces.

And boy, were they interesting.

Sickening, more like.

It was incredibly difficult to process that the billionaire was capable of such intense stalking, let alone murder. Veronica had seen a lot of awful shit in her lifetime, but she never would have anticipated this. To be frank, she never thought that he had it in him. *But once someone like him has so much impenetrable power...* she gritted her teeth in disgust. *I'm glad that son of a bitch got what was coming to him. Alien Girl must have run off for her own protection. Who knows what he tried to do to her?*

Images of Alien Girl panicking and vomiting in the back of the vehicle flashed in Veronica's mind.

So very human-like.

Both Alien Girl and Metaworld must be far more advanced than she ever knew. Perhaps...she had something like a human essence to her.

Why else would she murder her own creator?

Finally, Veronica scrolled down to the very last of the diary entries. Her eyes were immediately drawn to the most gruesome phrases within the text, making it impossible to read through the entries linearly.

"Cadaver prepared for surgery...continue her legacy...bring her here...real to me."

Her eyes widened.

He didn't.

Veronica had never clicked so quickly in her life before. She exited the text file and clicked on the folder named "PHOTOS." She rapidly went through all of the folders nested within it, only catching flashes of the thumbnails of all of the photo files dispersed throughout them, not wanting to look at them in any more detail out of fear of how sickened it would make her feel. Unfortunately, she was correct in her original suspicion.

He had murdered a woman and used her dead body to house Alien Girl's mind.

She got up from the computer and placed her head in her hands, trying to fight off an anxiety attack. The fact that he was dead now comforted her somewhat, but she couldn't prevent the intense feelings of fear and sickness that this new discovery made her feel.

Compose yourself, Veronica.

Get it together.

Shakily, she took a large external drive out of her backpack and inserted it into the computer. It automatically copied all of the files on it. It produced a small, almost polite sounding click whenever it was finished. She replaced it in her bag and started to climb her way back out of the mud-carved hallway.

"Xanthippe," her device crackled. Veronica jumped in fear over her transmission device suddenly going off. When her fear faded into embarrassment, she groaned. She elected to ignore their attempt to contact her until they realized their own mistake. Sure enough, they did after a few seconds had gone by.

"Darwin," they added sheepishly.

"Archipelago. Speak, Whiskey." Somehow, Veronica prevented her voice from betraying how shaken up she felt.

"We need you back soon. Over."

"Copy. Give me about one hour to return to vehicle. Found useful info. Over and out."

She sat on the grass above, her feet still dangling into the hole, and she pondered. She guessed that she could return to find Alien Girl after she went back to the mainland and went through all of the information she had discovered. For then, she could not afford to stick around on the island for too long.

Finally, she took a deep breath and stood up. She thought she would take a short walk along the coast before she took off. She needed to wash the paint from her skin before she returned. She didn't want to come back from a covert mission looking like a walking easter egg. That was asking for trouble. Aside from that, it was a lovely day. She needed a little bit of brain bleach before she made her journey back to the mainland.

When she arrived at the beach, she took off her shoes and felt the sand between her toes. Then she walked, lost in deep contemplation. *I dedicate a lot to my work,* she thought. *I think I deserve a small break before I go back.*

Veronica almost stepped into the ocean with her clothes on before she realized that she was the only living person around for miles. She walked back onto the shore and stripped down, deciding that she would take the opportunity to feel the sun on her skin and have dry clothes to put on after she was finished. When she walked back into the water, it felt nice and cool on her bare skin. She used her hands to scrub the paint off. The soothing sensation of the sea lapping at her body combined with the sun comfortably shining above her helped to calm her nerves. She began humming to herself again.

She walked far enough into the water so that it was chest high. In between washing the paint off, she half-walked, half-waded across the shoreline. The water was strikingly clear—even chest-deep, Veronica could see through it all the way to the bottom. She peered into the distance and admired the view.

As her eyes scanned the horizon, she noticed a human figure laid face-down on the sand, the waves lapping at its lower half. She froze.

Alien Girl.

Quickly, she waded back to the beach, running across the hot sand whenever she reached the surface again. She grabbed her backpack and sprinted toward the body.

"No, no, no, no, no," she frantically panted under her breath. *She can't be dead.*

It was a brutal sight. Just as she suspected, it was Alien Girl. *Or would it be more accurate to refer to her as Eclipta?*

Her mouth was gaping open. She was bloated and greyish, little pieces of her body here and there missing from different creatures feasting on it. Probably little crabs. The corpse only had one eye left, light and dull in color, peering up at the sky into nothingness. Her long hair was tangled and had the texture of wet straw.

Acting quickly, Veronica hunched over her backpack and pulled out a Swiss army knife. Luckily, she had recently sharpened all of the tools inside of it. She still doubted if it would work the way she needed it to. Nevertheless, she tried, not giving herself time to think about the gruesomeness of what she was about to do.

It was difficult not to. When she plunged her small saw-like tool into Alien Girl's head, it produced a sickening wet crunch that made bile travel up Veronica's throat. With difficulty, she suppressed the urge to vomit and got to work sawing around Alien Girl's skull. She prayed that what she was looking for would still be there.

Old, uncirculated blood gushed from the body's scalp. *Oh, Jesus,* Veronica thought.

Don't think too hard about it. Don't think too hard about it. Don't think too h-

She realized that the entire time she was sawing around Alien Girl's head, her eyes kept squeezing shut involuntarily. Not wanting to make any mistakes, she forced them to stay open. Her hands were completely coated in blood. The cross she wore around her neck was covered in blood, too. *Fuck, it better not be tarnished,* she thought miserably. *So much for brain bleach.*

When she had finally completed sawing a full circle around the top of the corpse's head, she yanked the scalp off by tugging on a handful of its hair. She whined under her breath. *Don't think too hard about it. Don't think about it at all.*

After she was finished, Veronica forced herself to look inside.

Eclipta's brain was still in there. Connected to it was a small, plastic black box with a slot on the side. She pulled the box out, trying not to feel too disgusted at its sickly visceral sheen, and pushed down on the slot's cover. A small computer chip popped out of it. In messy handwriting, it was labeled "Daisy."

"Daisy," Veronica whispered. Thankfully, it seemed to be in perfect condition. She pinched the chip between her fingers and carefully placed it in a small pocket in her backpack by itself. It would be safe there.

After wading back into the water to wash the blood off and getting dressed again, she walked back to the beach and looked down at the corpse. Sighing, she gently replaced its scalp and picked it up bridal style. She walked toward the thick forest near the shore. Veronica placed the body on the soft green grass and stared at it with pity. Eclipta was an unfortunate woman. The worst crime she ever committed was aligning too perfectly with the billionaire's taste and being in the wrong place at the wrong time. Rotten luck, really. After some thought, Veronica walked back to the Sanctuary. A while later, she returned with a shovel.

The grave that she created for Eclipta wasn't anything fancy. It was quite shallow, in fact. Unfortunately, she didn't have any time to provide something better. She was only able to make it deep enough for Eclipta to be placed inside without being visible once she was re-buried. *It's not like there's any large animals that will dig up her corpse, in the least,* Veronica thought.

When she finished placing shovelfuls of dirt back over Eclipta's body, she stared at the grave for a moment, unsatisfied. She glanced at a tree right behind it, got an idea, and pulled her Swiss army knife out. As neatly as she could, she carved something into its bark using big, scratchy capital letters.

"ECLIPTA."

When she was finished, she looked back down at Eclipta's grave again. She stayed that way for a few minutes. Nothing broke the silence except for a few bird calls. At last, she squatted down, patted Eclipta's grave, and walked back to her aircraft.

The whole walk back, something ate at Veronica. She made her decision when she finally reached the aircraft's doors.

She turned around and stared at the island, taking it all in one last time. Out of all the items she carried in her backpack, this was the one she least expected she would need.

Veronica pulled out her matchbook. Assuredly and steadily, she pulled one out and lit it in one swift motion. She walked over to a nearby pile of dry leaves in a dense collection of trees and dropped it in. The fire lit quickly. Soon, the flames would envelop the entire island. Nothing would be salvageable.

With one final glance at the crackling flame, quickly becoming a roaring inferno, she climbed back into her aircraft and flew away from the island. She did not look back.

Based in Oklahoma City and hailing from Denver, J.K. is a young author who writes poetry and fiction. They also enjoy music production, LGBT advocacy, swimming, and the visual arts.
At times, their prose gets as purple as the dark circles under their eyes.

Visit them at www.jkpetrie.com.

9 798869 069290